"You're not just a job, Vi."

Zach didn't look at her when he said it, and she knew the words hadn't been easy for him to get out. She gentled her tone. "I know. Thanks for everything."

"I'll get you settled in a [illegible] make sure everything's secure."

She stopped when he touched her shoulder.

"Really, Vi. Kidding aside. I want you to be careful."

A squealing of tires split the air. Zach's head jerked up. A car peeled around the curve, a flash of a familiar face behind the wheel—Roach. Another person filled the passenger window, big, barrel-chested, shaved head, just like Violet described.

Her attacker.

TRUE BLUE K-9 UNIT:

These police officers fight for justice
with the help of their brave canine partners

Justice Mission by Lynette Eason, April 2019
Act of Valor by Dana Mentink, May 2019
Blind Trust by Laura Scott, June 2019
Deep Undercover by Lenora Worth, July 2019
Seeking the Truth by Terri Reed, August 2019
Trail of Danger by Valerie Hansen, September 2019
Courage Under Fire by Sharon Dunn, October 2019
Sworn to Protect by Shirlee McCoy, November 2019
True Blue K-9 Unit Christmas
by Laura Scott and Maggie K. Black, December 2019

Dana Mentink is a national bestselling author. She has been honored to win two Carol Awards, a HOLT Medallion and an RT Reviewers' Choice Best Book Award. She's authored more than thirty novels to date for Love Inspired Suspense and Harlequin Heartwarming. Dana loves feedback from her readers. Contact her at danamentink.com.

Books by Dana Mentink

Love Inspired Suspense

True Blue K-9 Unit

Shield of Protection
Act of Valor

Gold Country Cowboys

Cowboy Christmas Guardian
Treacherous Trails
Cowboy Bodyguard
Lost Christmas Memories

Pacific Coast Private Eyes

Dangerous Tidings
Seaside Secrets
Abducted
Dangerous Testimony

Military K-9 Unit

Top Secret Target

Rookie K-9 Unit

Seek and Find

Visit the Author Profile page at Harlequin.com for more titles.

Act of Valor

Dana Mentink

HARLEQUIN® LOVE INSPIRED® SUSPENSE

Special thanks and acknowledgment are given to Dana Mentink for her contribution to the True Blue K-9 Unit miniseries.

Recycling programs for this product may not exist in your area.

ISBN-13: 978-1-335-67957-4

Act of Valor

This edition published by arrangement with Love Inspired Books.

www.Harlequin.com

Printed in U.S.A.

I will both lay me down in peace, and sleep:
for thou, Lord, only makest me dwell in safety.
—*Psalms* 4:8

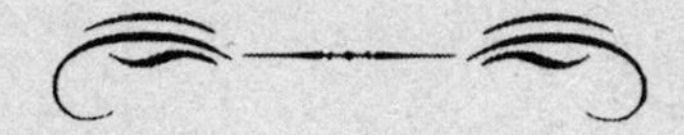

To the brave officers of the NYPD,
both canine and human, thank you for your service.

ONE

Instinct ratcheted up Violet Griffin's pulse. Something was definitely not right with the passenger who stood before her, his body stiff with impatience. The impatience part was par for the course at LaGuardia Airport in Queens. Her ticketing counter at Emerge Airline was always crazy, and passengers were not known for accepting delays with good cheer, but this guy was downright jumpy. Long and lean, with an ill-fitting canvas jacket, dark glasses and bottle-blond hair caught in a tight braid, he chewed his lip until it was his turn.

"I wanna talk to him, not you." The man pointed at her boss, Bill Oscar.

She took a moment to breathe, plaster on

her "you will not fluster me" mask and flip her curtain of wheat-brown curls behind her shoulder.

"No need. I can take care of you. May I see your driver's license please?"

He shifted the strap of the bag that hung from his shoulder. "I said I want your supervisor to check me in. That guy, over there."

She gritted her teeth, trying to keep her thoughts from coming out of her mouth. "I assure you, I can handle it, sir. I've been doing this job for a very long time."

"No," he snapped. "Him."

Shifting slightly, her fingers inched toward the security phone. If the man was about to become out of control, he'd be met with plenty of airport security.

But her boss flashed her a plump-cheeked smile. "I got this, Vi."

Insulted, she stepped aside and tended to another customer. Bill's easy grin was still in place. He must think her testiness was pure overreaction, since he did not seem the least bit nonplussed. Had he intervened to spare her aggravation, then? But she was an expert at dealing with aggravation and soothing ruffled feathers. She'd been doing it brilliantly for ten years now. She pondered her reaction to the guy as she processed a line of customers. Was her patience thinner than usual? Had her recent anguish started to show at work?

Zach Jameson's tormented blue eyes surfaced in her memory. He was in agony over the death of his older brother Jordan, the victim of a murder made to look like a suicide. She'd heard the officers gathered at her parents' diner reliving the terrible situation, trying to grapple with their grief. It had been torment for all the Jameson brothers, Noah, Zach and Carter, and for the entire NYC K-9 Command. Jordy had been the well-respected leader of their unit based in Queens. The loss was compounded by the fact that the guy who planted Jordan's fake suicide note had run into traffic and been killed while officers attempted to arrest him. The papers had run daily stories filled with more speculation than fact, but until the medical examiner's official findings were in, only Jordy's cop brothers knew for sure that their mentor had not killed himself, especially since his widow was expecting their first child.

Sadness and anger cloaked the whole NYC K-9 Command Unit in smothering grief, but it was the youngest Jameson brother who seemed to struggle most. She'd known Zach since she was a kid, and she prayed she could help him through the worst time in his life, but he was cold and distant, buried in a chill she could not penetrate no matter how hard she pressed.

Bill finished with the twitchy passenger and walked him across the busy floor to a security agent by the baggage screen. Violet relaxed. His carry-on bag would be x-rayed, and authorities alerted if anything was amiss. She was about to call out a thank-you to Bill when she saw the TSA agent usher the man through the line without putting his bag on the conveyor or walking him through the metal detector.

Agape, she hurried to her boss. “Bill, did you see that?”

He shuffled through the papers on his counter. “It’s not a problem. Don’t worry about it.” He gave his attention to the next customer.

Not a problem? How was allowing a passenger onto a plane without proper scan not a problem? Boss or no boss, she was about to let Bill have a piece of her mind when a voice snapped her back.

“I’m in a hurry.”

The next passenger’s license identified him as Joe Brown. The short, barrel-chested man was a regular, flying on business, she’d always assumed. The overhead lighting gleamed off his scalp, which shone through a harsh crew cut as he pushed his suitcase onto the scale.

"Your luggage is overweight, sir. You'll have to pay a fee."

He started to argue, but she merely pointed to the digital numbers on the scale. "Take something out and put it into your carry-on or pay the fee. That's it."

With a jerk, he plopped the suitcase down, putting his body between her and the contents, and yanked the zipper. She smelled the overpowering whiff of menthol. She leaned forward.

He stared at her, eyes like wet stones. "Cold rub. I've been ill."

Cold rub? Tension slithered through her stomach. She'd heard before from Zach that smugglers had all kinds of notions about how to fool the noses of detection dogs like Zach's beagle, Eddie. Cold rub…to mask the smell of…?

When the customer yanked a rolled-up leather jacket from his bag, she saw a glimpse of something inside, lumpy, wrapped in a sock. Whatever it was had some heft to it.

Her heart stopped. Cocaine? Should she call security? But what if she was misreading the situation like she might have with the previous passenger? She forced a nonchalant smile. "Excuse me for one minute."

She walked quickly to Bill and whispered to him. "I think that guy's smuggling drugs."

Bill frowned. "I'll take it from here."

She watched, pulse pounding in her throat as her boss approached Joe. The man stood quickly, pulled on the jacket, one side hanging down lower than the other. Whatever he'd had rolled inside must be jammed in the pocket now. She fingered her phone, ready to call for security or maybe even Zach. His work with a drug-detection dog took him all over Brooklyn and Queens as well as other boroughs, but currently he was assigned to LaGuardia Airport. She'd waved to him not an hour before, noting the slump of his shoulders, the haggard look that indicated another sleepless night.

To her utter shock, Bill Oscar pointed Joe toward the same security agent. This could not be. She grabbed at his sleeve, snapping at him. "What's going on?"

He detached himself. "Nothing at all. You need to relax. As a matter of fact, you're due for a break. I got the counter." He gently pressured her away. "Go get some coffee. You look tired."

He practically propelled her away, which only flipped on her stubborn switch. *No way. Whatever is going on here is not happening on my watch.* As Joe Brown strolled toward the TSA agent, she hurried along with her cell phone. If Bill was suddenly abdicating his job, she'd at least get a good picture of Brown and text it to Zach.

Just before she took the photo, Brown turned around.

His look brimmed with such malice, it was all she could do not to run. Her mouth went dry as she read the threat in the grim lines of his mouth. Backing away, she headed toward the employee break room, skin erupting in clammy goose bumps. The terminal was undergoing a remodel and the place where she was headed was sectioned off with cones—only employees allowed. Plastic draped the work areas and the din of an air compressor and a nail gun assaulted her eardrums.

Call Zach. Her fingers fumbled with the phone. The hairs on the back of her neck prickled, and she risked a look. Brown was striding toward her, putting himself between her and the milling crowd.

She realized her mistake at once.

Isolated corridor.

Empty break room.

And a drug smuggler bearing down on her.

She could scream, but over the din of the air compressor and construction noises no one would hear a sound.

It was time to run.

* * *

Officer Zach Jameson surveyed the throng of people congregated around the ticketing counter. Most ignored Zach and K-9 partner, Eddie, and that suited him just fine. Two months earlier he would have greeted people with a smile, or at least a polite nod while he and Eddie did their work of scanning for potential drug smugglers. These days he struggled to keep his mind on his duty while the ever-present darkness nibbled at the edges of his soul.

Jordan, his oldest brother and chief of the NYC K-9 Command Unit, was gone. Sometimes it still felt unreal to Zach. His words at his brother's funeral came back to him, when he'd promised Jordy's widow, Katie, that he and his brothers would bring her husband's killer to justice.

But they hadn't, not yet. It didn't help that his older brothers Noah and Carter, and other K-9 officers of the unit and all their collected dogs were officially off the case because of their familial connection to the victim. Even though Noah had been appointed interim chief, he was shut firmly out of the investigation like the rest of them. A storehouse of training, intelligence, loyalty and commitment and where had it gotten them? Nowhere. The only lead so far had been killed during the attempted arrest, and Zach had not even been on scene to try and prevent it. And to add one final twist to the knife in his gut, Jordy's police dog, Snapper, was still missing.

With Jordy gone, justice and duty were the only two things Zach had left, the former seeming more unreachable every passing day. As for duty, sometimes it felt like he was going through the motions in a haze—phoning it in, as his brothers might say. The badge meant everything to him, and he despised the way that grief was dulling his edge as a cop.

Eddie plopped his bony rump on Zach's

steel-toed boot and looked up into his face as if to say, "Let's do our jobs, okay?"

He stroked the dog's ears and sucked in a breath, trying to clear away the fog that had descended on him the moment he heard of his brother's death. A cop always lived with the fact that he might lose his life in the line of duty, but not this way, when Jordan and Katie had their first baby coming, and not when Zach should have been watching Jordan's back like Jordan had always done for his younger kin.

Jordan was the one who had prayed and prodded Zach through his police training, a process made more difficult by Zach's dyslexia. Everything hands-on came easy, but the written exams…taking those was like chiseling away at a mountain with a butter knife.

"Don't give up. Police force needs you, Zacho," Jordy had said during their tutoring sessions, employing the nickname Zach despised. "You're gonna be a great cop."

For all his brother's confidence, Zach hadn't had so much as a whiff of suspicion that his brother was in danger. Some cop, clueless and inept. His brain knew he should talk to somebody, somebody like Violet Griffin, his friend from childhood who'd reached out so many times. His brain knew, but his heart would not let him pass through the dark curtain. And there was no way he was talking to some department-appointed shrink who wasn't even a cop. They'd have to slap on cuffs and knock him unconscious before they dragged him into that office.

"Just get to work," he muttered to himself as his phone vibrated. Probably another text from his mom. Ivy Jameson paid no attention to the fact that he was not supposed to take personal messages while on duty. Truth be told, he'd been avoiding her calls because he could not stand to hear her cry or detect the worry in her voice when she asked him how he was doing. He'd call her later.

The phone trilled again, indicating it was a call this time. He checked the number.

Violet.

He considered ignoring it, but Violet didn't ever call unless she needed help and she rarely needed anyone. Strong enough to run a ticket counter at LaGuardia and have enough energy left over to help out at Griffin's, her family's diner. She could handle belligerent customers in both arenas and bake the best apple pie he'd ever had the privilege to chow down.

It almost made him smile as he accepted the call.

"Someone's after me, Zach."

Panic rippled through their connection. Panic, from a woman who was tough as they came. "Who? Where are you?"

Her breath was shallow as if she was running.

"I'm trying to get to the break room. I can lock myself in, but I don't… I can't…" There was a clatter.

"Violet?" he shouted.

But there was no answer.

He sprinted toward the Emerge Airline break room, Eddie racing right behind him.

TWO

Violet's phone spiraled out of her hand, clattering to the floor as Joe dropped his bag and grabbed for her arm. She wrenched herself free and lunged toward the break room door. Wild energy fueled her. When he caught up with her again, she fired a kick at his patella and heard his satisfying grunt of pain. He doubled over, grabbing at his knee, and she used the moment to thrust her ID card in its lanyard at the code reader. Her hands shook so badly it didn't work.

Why did you run here, you fool? The remodeling job left the normally bustling hallway quiet and deserted, no one to hear her scream, no one to help.

She shot a look over her shoulder. Brown

loomed behind her, cheeks flushed with exertion, nostrils flared, a grimace filled with violence with no human feeling behind it. There was no question in her mind that he would kill her if she gave him the slightest chance. Were there any construction workers or painters around? A single fellow employee?

Frantically, she tried her ID again, willing her fingers to cooperate. He was only a few yards away now, closing fast. After two agonizing seconds the door clicked open. She shoved it and scrambled inside, attempting to slam it behind her.

To her horror, something prevented it closing—Brown's booted foot. With everything in her she tried to hold the door closed, her arms rigid and trembling with the effort. Inch by inch he forced it open, one hand reaching through the gap, capturing her around the wrist, digging in.

Yanking free from his grip she scratched at his face, aiming for the eyes. Surprised, he jerked back. She threw all her body weight at the door. It shuddered but did not close. He rammed his boot at it and then he was in, pushing her until she fell backward onto the floor. Crab-walking in terror she looked for something, anything she could use to defend herself. She found nothing.

Towering over her, he smiled, one front tooth sporting a tiny chip. "You stuck your nose in where you shouldn't have."

"I called the cops," she said, throat tight. "They're on the way."

"You'll be dead before they get here." Again, the smile. "A quick death is better. We could make it last much longer if we wanted to."

She opened her mouth to scream, but he was on her, rough palm pressed over her mouth. Clawing and twisting she tried to break free, to make it to the door, to knee him, poke his eye, stop her own murder however she could.

He was too strong, deflecting her efforts

as though she were a small child instead of a grown woman fighting for her life.

He reached for his pocket.

She would kick out, roll away. Maybe she'd be shot or stabbed but she would go down fighting until she had not one tiny ounce of strength left.

She heard a shrill bark, the sound of scrabbling claws and running feet. He grabbed her chin in his hand, fingers pressing into her flesh. "You butted in to my business. Not gonna leave any witnesses behind to ID me. This won't be done until you're dead." Then he released his grip and charged to the door.

Through her shuddering breaths, she heard another bark. It was Eddie, had to be, and Zach. Would they be gunned down as they sprinted toward the break room? Frantically, she tried to scramble to her feet, but her body systems were offline, legs trembling, lungs gasping for breath, terror charging every nerve and sinew. The best she could do was sit up, head whirling.

Zach slammed through the door with Eddie, gun in hand. Relief made her whimper. Brown must have gotten away without a shoot-out.

When he saw her, his blue eyes went wide and he dropped to a knee at her side. Eddie whined and poked his nose at her shin.

"Vi…how bad is it?"

"I…" she stammered. He was reaching for the radio clipped to his shoulder.

"Don't move. I'm calling an ambulance. Backup is already rolling, and Carter will be here in two minutes."

"No," she finally managed. He stopped as if he'd gotten an electric shock.

"I'm okay." She finally got the words out.

"No, you're not. I'm calling."

She forced her teeth to stop chattering. "Go after him, Zach. He goes by Joe Brown. He had drugs in his suitcase. I saw. He's wearing a brown leather jacket."

"Not leaving you."

Zach reached for the radio again, but she snatched for his wrist, pressing her fingers there and taking comfort in the steady rhythm of his pulse.

"I'm okay. Not hurt."

He raised a doubtful eyebrow. "You'd say that if you'd been sawed in half."

She shoved the hair from her face. "New York tough."

He touched her cheek with a tentative finger. "Griffin tough. You have a red mark. Here."

The touch made something ache inside, but she brushed him off. "Go do your job," she said in a voice with only the tiniest break in it, which she hoped he would not notice. "There was another guy. I don't know if they were together. He had a long braid. My boss, Bill, he escorted him to security and the TSA let him through without scanning his bags."

"Vi..." He huffed out a breath, broad

chest still heaving from his run along the corridor. "Let me help you, wouldja? You could be hurt more than you think."

She flashed him a cocky smile. "Griffin tough, remember?"

She knew what he was thinking. Jordan, his hero of an older brother, had been tough, too, and now he was dead. Zach's expression said it all.

With surprising tenderness, he pressed his cheek to her palm. Warmth spread from their point of contact, up her arm, reviving and restoring. She wanted to keep him there, strong jaw, warm skin, the gesture so vulnerable. She yearned to reach out and stroke his thatch of close-cut chestnut hair and block out what had just happened.

"I'm not losing any more family. Not on my watch," he mumbled into her cupped palm.

Family. You're like a sister to him, her mind prodded. *That's all.* She sucked in a breath and tried to get hold of her glitching emotions. It took all her effort to detach herself from him. "I'm fine. Like I said. Stop babying me."

Another officer barreled in. Zach brought him up to speed and the officer relayed the info on the radio.

Zach shifted his attention from his colleague to her and back again.

"Go," she said, tone all business, tipping her chin up and daring him with her glance to disobey.

He gave her one more look, filled with emotions that a tough K-9 cop would never put into words. Concern for a longtime family friend, no doubt. Eagerness to do his job. Guilt at how he'd failed his brother. His gaze wandered her face, lips twitching for a moment with some unspoken thought. Her heart ached to see something else in his countenance, something beyond duty and childhood affection, but he turned away, in pursuit of his quarry.

Part of her prayed he would catch up to Joe Brown.

This won't be done until you're dead.

The other part prayed he wouldn't.

Fifteen frustrating minutes later Zach met his brother Carter by the ticket counter. The suspect had bolted. Zach noted the disgruntled white shepherd, Frosty, panting at Carter's side. Fortuitous that Carter, a transit K-9 cop, was at LaGuardia for some training with the TSA employees. The command unit had dogs assigned to various departments throughout the NYPD so most of the time they were not serving in the same spot at the same time. They each had their specific unit duties, which could be preempted if a situation required a particular canine's abilities. The duties were ever changing, and it was part of the reason Zach loved his job. Even before Carter's report, Zach could tell by the dog's dejected demeanor that there had been no suspect taken into custody. Zach felt exactly the same way as the dog. He ground his teeth as his brother spun out the details.

"Witnesses saw a guy matching the description exit the airport heading west. We're on it. Still trying to work out what happened to the other guy. He didn't get on a plane, so he must have seen the cop activity and taken off, too." He cocked his head. "Vi?"

"She says she's okay. Refused an ambulance."

Carter quirked a wry smile. "Yeah. Big surprise. I'll gather Violet's boss and any other witnesses we can round up. You and Eddie gonna do a sweep?"

"Yeah. Listen, can you pull someone else to start on the statements and go sit with Violet? She's shaken up, and I want one of us with her."

His brother nodded. "Ten-four. On my way."

It made Zach feel infinitely better to know

that Carter would be with Violet. For all her brave talk, there was a shadow of something in her eyes that made him wonder if she was as okay as she proclaimed to be. Not that she'd admit anything else under pain of death.

Considering the lowlife who put his hands on her made Zach's blood heat to near boiling. He forced himself to calm down. Tension was transmitted right down the leash, through the harness to Eddie, and there was no need for that. Eddie had had a difficult start in life, tied to a streetlamp as a puppy one bitter February evening and left to die. Sent to a busy shelter, he'd been rescued by a group that evaluated dogs for potential police service. Eddie's nose, even as an untrained pup, was stellar. He'd been given his name in honor of fallen NYPD officer Ed Owens. Best of all, Eddie worked for two things: affection and treats. Zach made those treats from scratch. Nothing was too good for Eddie.

Zach bent down and fondled Eddie's ears, capturing the dog's muzzle and looking at his sad brown eyes. "You're my good baby, aren't you?" he whispered in a singsong voice that he'd never allow anyone else to hear. Then, louder, "Work time."

Eddie sprang to his feet, twenty-five pounds of get-up-and-go, primed for the search. If Violet was right, maybe her attacker had ditched the drugs somewhere when he heard the cavalry arrive. If there were drugs in the vicinity, Eddie would know it, thanks to his 220 million scent receptors and a ferocious drive to do his job. All that dog talent wrapped in an adorable package. Eddie was a rock star, in Zach's view, even if he had a two-mile-wide stubborn streak. *Just like his handler*, Jordy had often said.

"Find the drugs, Eddie."

The dog put his nose to the floor as they worked their way along the corridor. There was nothing of interest immediately outside the break room. Eddie snuffled along the corridor with that signature beagle trot and tail wag. They headed to the terminal, which the cops had temporarily closed. Irate passengers huffed and complained. He ignored them, easing Eddie through the throng. Another beautiful thing about beagles: they didn't scare people like some other breeds of police dogs. Eddie was a goodwill ambassador when he wasn't taking down drug smugglers.

Carter messaged him that they had still not located the first guy who had passed through security. He'd somehow vanished, leading Zach to believe he'd been helped out of the airport by the same crooked employee and possibly Violet's boss.

Eddie sniffed, nose glued to the floor. Nothing. He shook his ears.

"Come on, boy. Anything?"

They moved on a few paces.

With a cheerful swish of his tail, Eddie waggled his way toward a cleaning cart.

The custodian was about to empty a dustpan into the big plastic garbage bin.

An invisible shock went through the dog. Eddie tensed, tail erect, nostrils quivering. Zach could practically feel the animal's excitement, or maybe it was his own. He tried to keep his breathing even as Eddie circled and sat, the perfect passive response signal. He looked up at Zach.

"Sir, can you hold up a minute?" Zach called.

The custodian jerked in surprise. "Huh?"

"I need you to stop what you're doing for a moment."

The guy nodded and stepped away from the trash can. Zach peered in. "May I?" Zach said, pointing to a box of rubber gloves on the cart.

"Knock yourself out."

Zach pulled on rubber gloves and reached into the can, hauling out the brown leather jacket Violet had described and trying not to crow his triumph. Now he had physical evidence. There might be hair, prints, clues. Zach would bust the dirtbag who'd put his hands on Violet. It wasn't as good as chasing him down and cuffing him, but it was enough for now.

The custodian's mouth fell open. "Why would somebody throw away a perfectly good jacket?"

Zach put the pieces into place. Joe Brown was in a hurry, he'd heard Eddie approaching, a dog tracking the scent of the drugs, and he was desperate not to be caught. Eddie bayed long and loud. A sock peeked out of the jacket pocket, reeking with the smell of menthol rub. "He took the drugs out of his suitcase and dumped the jacket as a diversion when he ran," Zach muttered.

The custodian whistled. "Ain't that something. He figured your dog couldn't track the scent of drugs because of the cold rub?"

Zach gave Eddie one of his homemade treats from a pouch at his waist. "He figured wrong."

THREE

Zach waited impatiently for the airport officers to secure the evidence before he practically jogged with Eddie to find Violet. She looked more herself now, sitting in one corner of the employee room while Carter and the TSA supervisor interviewed her boss, Bill Oscar, in the other. He could tell by the tapping of her sleek pump on the carpeted floor that she was itching to confront the man herself. He went to her.

"Are you okay?"

"Yes, of course. He just knocked me over, that's all. Did you…?"

"He made it out of the terminal, but we've got officers looking for him, canvassing bus and subway stations, alerting the taxi cabs, et cetera. We'll get him."

"What about the other guy? Bill walked him to security. I don't know if he boarded or not."

"Looks like he ran, too. We're going over the camera footage. Don't worry."

She caught her lip between her teeth in that way that meant she was thinking. Violet was smart, so much smarter than he'd ever be. She'd been working on a college business degree in the evenings before her father broke his ankle last summer. Then she'd stepped in to help at the family restaurant, putting aside her college work for a while. Though her school was on a break for the next two weeks, she'd reenrolled in classes again, determined to finish this time. Smart, steel-tough, sassy, loyal as the day was long; that was Violet Griffin.

Bill finished with the officer and walked to them. "I am glad you're okay, Vi. I was worried."

A shower of sparks lit her eyes from coffee to caramel. "Don't bother with the pleasantries. You let the guy with the braid bypass security and you would have done the same with Joe Brown if I hadn't intervened. What gives?"

He shook his head. "Absolutely not. You misunderstood what you saw. I didn't know that TSA agent was gonna pass him through." He looked at Zach. "The guy with a long braid, acting shifty. I walked him to security personally. I figured he'd be scanned and detained if there was cause. That's a TSA responsibility."

"Just ID'd him from security footage. Roger Talmadge, goes by Roach. He's got a rap sheet—petty stuff, DUI, possession," Zach said.

Bill nodded. "I delivered him right to screening but there must have been something shady between this Roach and the TSA guy."

"Yeah," Zach said. "Agent's name is Jeb Leak. At the moment, he's missing."

"See?" Bill sighed. "On the take. New

guy. I should have suspected, but…" He shrugged. "Well frankly, I was preoccupied. The wife's been sick, you know, and she's got a checkup today to see how the treatment's been working." His forehead was creased with deep grooves. "She's been in the hospital more than she's been out."

Though it looked as if her ire dulled a fraction, Violet was not about to be appeased. "What about Joe Brown? He had drugs in his suitcase. I saw it before he moved it to his pocket, and the chest rub was extra protection against the dogs."

"I agreed with you. He was probably smuggling something." Bill fixed her with a look. "Vi, you're killing me. We've worked together for ten years now, and I didn't want you involved if things were gonna get ugly, which is why I walked him there myself, just like the first guy. I was trying to protect you and you're practically accusing me of being in cahoots with a smuggler. How could you possibly think that?"

Violet didn't reply.

"Dump the guilt trip. Your behavior was suspicious," Zach said. "She was right about both men."

"I was trying to do my job and keep her out of trouble. I'd think that would garner a little appreciation." He sighed. "If you two are done interrogating me, I've got a mess of people at the ticket counter to sort through."

Violet started to follow him.

"No, no," Bill said, holding up a hand. "You go on home now. You've had a bad day and Liz is here to start her shift. Go get some rest."

Vi watched him leave, a troubled crimp on her mouth.

"You believe him?" Zach asked.

"I've known them for a long time. His wife, Rory, has been sick—breast cancer—and she hasn't responded well to treatments. He's shouldered a lot of the load with his two boys. Maybe he really was preoccupied, trying to keep me out of it." She broke off to look at Zach. "Do you trust him?"

"I'm not wired to trust people. Occupational hazard, but I do agree with him that you should go home. I'll take you."

She brushed back her hair with an impatient hand. "I don't need a chaperone. I can take the bus home or call a car service."

He braced himself for battle. "My car's faster. I have a shiny red siren."

"Your seats smell like a wet beagle, and you have a shift to finish. Go back to work."

He folded his arms. "My vehicle was detailed yesterday, and Eddie has recently been bathed with special shampoo. He practically reeks with the scent of a spring meadow. I'm walking you to my car and driving you home. You don't get to have a say in that, so grab your bag and let's go."

Her nostrils flared. "You're pushy."

"I'm right, as usual."

Vi arched an eyebrow. "Pretty high-and-mighty for a guy who can't ride a bike and breaks things on a regular basis."

"I can ride a bike, I just don't want to, and it's been two whole days since I busted anything."

"Uh-huh, but the last one at the diner was a doozy. You knocked over a wait stand and broke six dishes and a coffeepot."

"Four. Your mother said it was four dishes."

"My mother lied to make you feel better. I'm not as kind as she is."

"Get your bag, Vi," he said with a chuckle. He felt her staring at him. "What is it now?"

A gentle smile lit her face. "You laughed. I haven't heard you laugh since..." The smile faded. "I mean...for weeks."

He lifted a shoulder and grabbed for Eddie's leash. Violet had always been able to make him laugh with that combination of edgy humor and intelligence, matching him tease for tease. He knew a lot of great women—pretty, smart, ambitious—dated many of them, but none like her. There was something just...*better* about her, which he could not pin down. Probably she seemed different because he'd known her since she was a gap-toothed first-grader. Still, Violet was irreplaceable and if he and God were on speaking terms, he'd say a prayer of thanks that she was unharmed. Anger bit hard at him.

He and God weren't friends anymore. Zach deserved to encounter shipwrecks in his life, he'd probably caused most of them with his combination of impulsivity and stubbornness, but Jordy... God should have looked out for Jordy. No, he and God were no longer on speaking terms.

Shoving on his hat, he strode out of the room, grateful to have Vi clipping along in her pumps right next to him.

Violet kept her pace quick in spite of the twinges in her back and her throbbing cheekbone. She would not let Zach see her discomfort, especially the inner turmoil simmering below the surface like a monster fish ready to suck her under. She didn't want to speak of her feelings, not the real, raw, deep-down ones. Not to Zach.

He has too much on his heart already. I can't add to his burdens. Besides, they had their roles: he the jokester, overprotective big-brother type, and she the in-control, stand-up-to-anyone tough girl. She intended to keep it that way for both their sakes.

Bad enough that everyone was no doubt waiting at the diner, talking about what had happened. Her father would press for her to move into the cramped bedroom at the house in Rego Park where she'd grown up, but that would be going backward and she would not allow herself to give in to the fear. The airport attack was upsetting, traumatic, but it wasn't going to derail her progress. Her college classes were starting up again in a matter of weeks, and this time she wasn't going to take a break until she had that business degree firmly in her possession.

She was grateful that Zach did not seem to be in a talking mood as they exited the terminal and climbed on a shuttle. They made their way to the parking structure where Zach's car occupied a reserved police spot. Inside the garage the gloom felt smothering, the acrid scent of gasoline and exhaust making her stomach flip over. Eddie shook his muzzle as if to clear away the barrage of odors.

The silence grew tedious as they stepped into the garage elevator. She noticed the steely look on Zach's face. Claustrophobic, though he staunchly denied it. It brought her back to a day when the two of them, teenage rebels cutting school to go to the beach, had discovered a massive drainage pipe and stupidly gone in to explore. The deeper they'd gone into that cement tube, the sweatier and more panic-stricken Zach had become until she'd thought he was going to pass out. Grabbing his wrist, she'd led him from the pipe to a spot of sand where she'd held him around the shoulders until his breathing quieted.

"Sorry, Vi," he'd said, mortified, forehead pressed to hers.

She'd squeezed his fingers, kissed him on the cheek, made a joke and never mentioned the incident again. It was her gift to him, a secret kept, a silent pact from two childhood friends. And he'd kept her secrets, too. In eighth grade Gil Fisher had stolen her journal from her locker. Violet wasn't a writer, but inside were her sketches of the boys she'd had crushes on, complete with colored hearts around them. Gil was prepared to share her private drawings with every kid in the school until Zach got a hold of him. Whatever he'd said to Gil she would never know, but Gil had promptly handed back the journal and none of them had ever spoken of it. She wondered for the millionth time if Zach had seen the last picture in the journal, a picture she'd sketched of him.

As the elevator shuddered upward, the tight line of his jaw indicated that he was gritting out the ride. She wished she had the nerve to take his hand again and tell him she still understood, had his back through whatever would come. She yearned to comfort him about Jordy's death. How the touch would comfort her, too, still the wobbling in her stomach and the trembling in her knees. But they had roles to play, didn't they? Instead, she watched the buttons light the way to the third floor and stepped out next to him.

Violet sighed. "Satisfied? We made it to your car safe and sound. Box checked. The first part of your job is done."

He frowned. "You're not just a job, Vi."

He didn't look at her when he said it, and she knew the words hadn't been easy for him to get out. She gentled her tone. "I know. Thanks for everything."

"I'll get you settled in at your apartment. Make sure everything's secure."

"Not necessary."

"Did you get an alarm system or a Doberman since I was there last?"

"No."

"Then I'll check the doors and windows, since your roomie's out of town."

She threw up a hand. "Okay. You win."

"That's a first."

"It probably won't happen again anytime soon."

"Then I'll just bask in the glow."

She stopped at the rear bumper when he touched her shoulders.

"Really, Vi. Kidding aside. I want you to be careful." His hands wandered up her back, coming to rest on her neck under her hair. The blue of his eyes lulled her, his face so incredibly handsome.

A squealing of tires split the air. Zach's

head jerked up. A car peeled around the curve, a flash of a familiar face behind the wheel, big, barrel-chested.

Her attacker.

Joe Brown.

Eyes slitted, ruthless, determined half smile.

The car bore down on them. Zach shoved Violet behind him.

In terror she grappled to get hold of his shirt and pull him back with her between the parked cars, but he was turning, reaching for his side arm, shouting.

The car careened on, charging toward Zach and Eddie like a heat-seeking missile until the front bumper plowed into the rear of Zach's SUV.

Glass shattered somewhere close, pinging her with tiny chips. She stumbled.

Zach leaped backward, pulling Eddie with him, crashing into the side of the vehicle. A bright drop of blood splattered the rear passenger window.

Zach lay on the ground, eyes closed, while Eddie whined and pawed at his chest.

FOUR

Zach felt pressure on his rib cage, a flash of hot pain on his cheek, followed by the clammy squelch of a probing dog nose. Cold from the cement floor seeped through his uniform shirt. The sensations coalesced all at once into a frantic need to move. He opened his eyes and jerked to a sitting position, sending Eddie into another round of high-pitched yelping. He saw himself mirrored in Violet's brown irises as she stared down at him. She pressed a hand to his sternum.

"Stay still. I'll call for an ambulance."

He ignored her, struggling to his feet while scanning the parking lot for Joe Brown. He was long gone. Zach bit back a growl of frustration, jerked his radio free and called in. The on-duty police and TSA were alerted to look for the vehicle. It was the best they could do. He declined medical help, of course. Mercifully, Violet appeared unharmed. One thing had gone right, anyway.

"How did he know you were leaving with me?" he mused. "Seems unlikely he would stick around to tail us." It wasn't coincidence, either. LaGuardia had multiple police parking areas, both outdoors as well as the garage, so it hadn't been a fortunate guess on the part of Brown. They might have been followed from the terminal, but he probably would have noticed that and no one had tracked them into the elevator.

Violet frowned and he knew what she was thinking.

"Your boss knows you left with me?"

She hesitated. "Yes."

"So it would be easy for him to pass that on to Brown..."

"He wouldn't do that," Violet said, but she didn't sound convinced. He wasn't, either.

Carter's text buzzed in his phone.

Anyone hurt?

Violet's okay.

You?

Just my pride.

He put the phone away before Carter got a chance to snap off a snarky reply.

Violet was pulling at his wrist, turning him to face her. "No matter how they found out, they're gone and you're bleeding. Stay still."

"No, I'm not hurt."

"Yes," she said in the overly controlled voice she used when he was driving her to distraction. "You are." She pointed to the side of his head.

He felt then a trickle of warmth and

swiped at it, his fist coming away with a smear of red. "I'm not hurt," he repeated, hoping he didn't sound like a cranky child.

She grabbed a tiny packet of tissues from her purse and pressed one to his temple, pulling it away to show him the blood. "Not-hurt people don't bleed on other people's clothes."

He noticed another spot on the front of her uniform.

"Sorry," he mumbled. "I must have hit the door handle on the way down. I'll wash it."

"No, you'll have it dry-cleaned, you big oaf," she said, but her smile was soft as she dabbed at his cut. "Doesn't look deep. Cops will send a unit to check on you, or an ambulance, right?"

"Told 'em not to. Need every cop out looking for Brown."

She heaved out a sigh. "And you say *I'm* stubborn."

"You are. Way more stubborn than me."

The rumble of an engine caught her attention. "Fortunately, it looks as if someone didn't listen to you, though."

Carter pulled up in his squad car, Frosty pacing in the backseat. "Get in, Zach."

Zach shook his head. "Uh-uh. I'm taking Vi back to her apartment."

Carter used the same tone he did when his young daughter Ellie was refusing to cooperate. "No, you're getting into this car until our people process this scene, and we're taking Vi to Griffin's. Everyone's there and waiting."

Violet took Zach's hand, put it over the tissue and pressed both to his head. "Do as you're told."

He wanted to snap at her and his brother, to vent some of the tension that threatened to explode. Instead, he forced out a long, slow breath. "Fine."

Carter jerked his head. "You're sitting in the back with Frosty. Vi gets the front seat."

She cocked her head and flashed that smile again, but there was something forced about the brashness, as if she was trying a little too hard to hide her fear. It made him crazy to see it.

Don't worry, Vi. I'm gonna get these guys no matter what it takes.

Hauling himself and Eddie into the cramped backseat of Carter's vehicle, he heard the echo of another promise, the one he'd made to Jordy's widow, the promise that he'd catch Jordy's killer no matter what it took. As the days spun into weeks with no progress from the cops working the case, his frustration was building to epic levels. At least the rabid press coverage had eased a bit, his brother's "suicide" taking backseat to various other big-city stories.

Everyone who worked with Jordy already knew it wasn't a suicide, but given the suicide note that had been planted and the lack of outward trauma to his body, that didn't keep the press from their speculations. He realized his jaw was clamped like a vise and he made an effort to relax.

Maybe it would be good to have Violet to focus on while they continued to try and unearth a lead on his brother's killer. The fatigue of many sleepless nights crowded the adrenaline from his muscles. Wearily, he stroked Eddie, threading his fingers through the fur, allowing himself just for a moment to wonder if Jordy's dog, Snapper, might still be alive. There had been blood found in Jordy's SUV, animal blood, but not a single trace of Snapper anywhere. If the German shepherd was wandering loose, lost, injured, how long could he survive?

A wave of despair washed over him. Zach used to believe there was nothing he couldn't do, that God was watching over the Jameson family and the people they loved.

I will both lay me down in peace, and sleep: for thou, Lord, only makest me dwell in safety. The psalm was inscribed inside the Bibles his mother had given each of them the day they were sworn in as cops. Now he couldn't even read the words without choking on them. With Jordy's death, there was no more peace or rest, and now with Violet facing a different threat, there would be no fairy-tale promises of safety, either.

I'll do it without You, he silently promised, the stone where his heart used to be hardening with each syllable. *I'll keep her safe.* It felt good to direct his anger at God, who'd taken the very best friend he'd ever had.

You won't take anyone else from me.

Carter shot him a look in the rearview mirror as they turned onto 94th Street and passed the K-9 headquarters, eventually pulling up in the tiny lot behind Griffin's Diner. Violet got out and beelined for the door.

Carter cut the motor and turned to stare at Zach. "You okay?"

"Yeah." He shifted Eddie on his lap. "Why?"

"Because you look like you're ready to take on an army all by yourself."

"Maybe I will."

Carter shook his head. "That's not smart. We're a team. Don't go rogue on us."

Zach didn't speak, but his gut filled in the answer.

If that's what it takes to protect Vi, bring it on.

"Zach," Carter started again, but Zach was already out and following Violet into the comfort of the diner.

Violet breathed deeply of the familiar aromas, the rich tang of coffee, the scent of the freshly waxed floors her father insisted on, the tantalizing fragrance of simmering soup with glistening homemade noodles and shredded chicken, never diced. It was the smell of home, of comfort, of safety. The place had been unchanged for decades, obstinately resisting the pressure of the encroaching neighborhood gentrification of Jackson Heights. Her father would inevitably turn red in the face when he passed the two new luxury rental buildings and the artisanal cheese shop that had replaced the old mom-and-pop stores. Griffin's was rooted in the history of Queens, standing defiantly against the so-called progress, preserving the character of the people who had built the neighborhood brick by brick, block by block.

Sucking in a lungful of diner smells, she put the fear behind her and automatically snatched her apron from the hook by the door.

"Oh, no, you don't," her mother said. Barbara Griffin was still tall and straight-backed in spite of the lifetime of sweat and tears she'd put into the diner and raising Violet. Some silver threaded her brown hair, which she wore wound into the trademark braid. She'd never know how her mother survived losing Violet's brother at age five to meningitis, but Barbara was strong, and she'd passed that strength down to her daughter.

Sometimes you build a wall around today and you don't climb over it, her mother had told her. Violet was determined to build a wall around the frightening events of the morning and keep them behind the bricks, away from the rest of her life.

Her mother embraced her quickly, hard and tight, the contact telling her all that she couldn't say in words. After a breath, she straightened. "Carter filled me in. Are you sure you're okay?"

"Yes, Mom," she said, pulling the apron around herself. The apron made her feel safer than a suit of armor. "I'm completely fine. I'll bus table seven."

"I'd like to see you try," she said, smiling. "You'll have to get around your dad first." Violet decided that nothing would stop her, but when she made it to the dining room, the place was swimming with cops. They were collected around their favorite tables in their private room, set apart by French doors and affectionately dubbed "The Dog

House," grilling Zach for the details. On the walls of the cozy room were the photos of those NYPD officers who had lost their lives in the line of duty. The K-9s were given the names of these fallen heroes to keep their memories alive. With a pang she realized that Jordy's picture would soon be added to those photos. The dogs were settled into their private porch area, and Zach led Eddie in to join them. Zach's brothers, Carter and Noah, were there with their dogs, and siblings Reed and Lani Branson along with Luke Hathaway, Brianne Hayes, Tony Knight and Gavin Sutherland. They were not all related by blood, but all were part of the K-9 unit Jordy Jameson had supervised, so that made them as close as kin could be.

She was about to grab the coffeepot and start pouring out for the cops when her father hastened up, quick though he sported a potbelly, and wrapped her in a hug that lifted her off the ground. "Baby," he said.

"What is this world coming to? That airport is full of crazy people. You could have been killed. I think you should come back here and work full-time. Forget the airline job."

She squeezed him in return, furiously blinking back tears. "You always say that, Daddy."

"And I always mean it." He cupped her face and kissed her on the nose like he'd done since she could remember. One of her earliest memories was her and her little brother Bobby dressed up for Easter morning, her father presenting them each with a kiss on the nose and a basket full of goodies. Lou Griffin was a softie, through and through.

Before she could protest, he steered her to the back room into an empty chair at the table full of cops. "You're my baby, and I need you to be safe. Sit down and rest."

"I just got here."

"Rest from your ordeal. No waiting tables for you."

Her mother chuckled, carrying in pitchers of ice water. “See? I told you.”

Everyone broke into a vigorous inquisition about her health and safety with a liberal amount of teasing thrown in. Holding on to her tough and independent demeanor was hard when she spoke of the attack, but she kept herself in check. She was Violet Griffin, known for her sass and wit, a strong woman who wasn’t going to present anything else to her cop family, and they knew it, counted on it. When the conversation turned to shoptalk, she breathed an inward sigh.

“We got the intel back on the Joe Brown guy,” Carter said. “His real name is Xavier Beck. Small-time, petty theft, some drug arrests. He may be a courier, but he’s not the boss. Though there’s been some street chatter that he’s moving up in the ranks, trying to prove himself. We’ve heard the name Uno.”

“You think he’s the guy in charge?” Zach pressed.

Noah shrugged. “Nothing definitive, but

it's telling that when we bring up the name, all our sources close up tighter than a tick on a coonhound. There's something behind this guy Uno."

"Another drug ring putting down roots here in Queens?" her father asked with a shake of his head.

"Plenty of noise that there's a drug-smuggling operation organizing," Carter said, "but we can't prove this Uno character is behind it. Malcolm Spade was running things until recently, but thanks to Declan, we got him put away."

Declan Maxwell was Zach's longtime friend and the newest K-9 officer with the elite NYPD Vapor Wake Squad. Along with the Jameson brothers, Jordan among them, Declan and his dog Storm had helped take down the drug kingpin. Thinking about it set loose a wave of sadness inside her. She had not seen Katie, Jordan's pregnant wife, at the diner in several weeks. Zach's grimace made her believe he'd been thinking about his lost brother also.

"What about the TSA guy?" Noah asked.

"No sign of him but we're looking."

Zach toyed with his coffee mug. "Bill Oscar's got to be involved. I'm going to put him under a microscope and tear his past apart until I get to the bottom of it."

Violet bit her lip. Her heart told her Bill was a good boss, a good father, a good friend, but there was no way to overlook the fact that he'd acted suspiciously at the airport. Zach's flinty expression told her she had zero chance of diverting him from that course of the investigation, anyway.

"You shouldn't go back to your apartment," Zach said, fixing her with eyes darkened to navy. "It's not safe. If Bill's involved, he can feed Beck your address."

There was universal agreement around the table.

"He wouldn't..." she started to say, until uncertainty dried up the words.

"She can move in with us," Barbara said. "Help take care of that little stinker of a puppy."

The pup's mother, Stella, was a gift from the Czech Republic to the NYPD. The yellow Lab had surprised one and all by having eight puppies shortly after her arrival, leaving the department scrambling for homes for all the pups. K-9 officer Brianne Hayes was now training mama Stella in the ways of bomb detection, but her babies were unharnessed hurricanes needing constant supervision. Latte, the precocious pup, had found a home with the Griffins. Two others had been placed with Carter and his daughter Ellie in the Jameson home. Violet figured them to be a welcome distraction in the wake of Jordy's murder.

"Yeah, you're gonna need another set of hands at least," Carter said with a groan. "The two we've got are tearing up the place. I'm down a gym bag and a Yankees cap already. Ellie is all set to keep them forever, even though they've mangled her toy sewing machine."

"So everyone agrees, then," her father said. "It's settled. Violet can work here and stay at our place. I need help keeping up with the pie demand, and everyone says that your pies are superior, Violet. Your mother's got a little birthday shindig here on Tuesday afternoon, remember. She's expecting big stuff in the pie department."

Violet steeled herself. Her father would be content if she never left their family dwelling in Rego Park, right next door to the Jamesons' shared family home. She was never sure if his overprotectiveness was due to losing his son, or the fact that she was a female, or just his natural bent, but whatever the reason, she'd fought for her independence and she wouldn't let it be stripped away because of Xavier Beck. "Hold up just one minute. As much as I adore you all, no one is going to organize my life. I am perfectly fine at my apartment, and I'm not giving up my job at the airport."

"But..." her father started.

"It's not safe," Zach said again. He got to his feet. Eddie eyed him from the porch room and stood, too, tail wagging in anticipation of a departure. "This guy Beck knows you saw the drugs in his bag. You can testify. You shouldn't be alone."

She stood. "I'm not alone. I have a roommate."

He was unmoved. "Who is away on an overseas assignment for another three weeks, correct?"

"Yes, but I live in a building with a hundred other tenants. The guy next door is a butcher, and he knows how to handle a meat cleaver, if it comes to that."

Her father snorted. "He works practically round the clock, plus he's a Red Sox fan and that just speaks to his poor character right there." He threw up his hands as if he'd just set the universe in order.

Violet stood as tall as she could manage. Good thing she was wearing heels. Even so, she had to tip her head to look Zach in the eye. “With or without a butcher next door, I am a very competent woman, thank you very much.”

“Vi...” Zach towered over her, handsome face close enough for her to reach out and touch the fatigue lines that grooved his forehead. She kept her hands clenched by her sides. “This isn’t about competence,” he said wearily.

The softness in his voice almost broke her resolve. Bossiness she could deal with, but tenderness... She swallowed. “I will not be forced out of my home. I’m safe and I’m not scared.” She tried to believe her own brash statement.

They all stared at her. Zach folded his arms across his chest. It seemed like the entire diner went dead silent.

Noah cleared his throat. “We’ll assign a detail to watch her place.”

Zach shook his head. “No. It’s not enough. Vi, I want you to stay with your parents.”

Right next door to the home he shared with his brothers? It was part of the reason she’d been so anxious to move away. It killed her an inch at a time to see him every day, watch him bringing his girlfriends to the house for family dinners, to try and pretend she was happy for him when her own heart was protesting. In the months before Jordy was killed, she thought she’d actually achieved some level of normalcy, accepting that Zach and the Jamesons had their own lives and loves that didn’t involve her. *It’s the way he wants it*, she’d finally convinced herself. She thrust her chin up. “Badge or not, you don’t get to tell me what to do, Zach.”

His eyes sparked, narrowed, pinned her in that way he probably did when he was staring at someone he was about to arrest. She stared right back, hoping the fire in her eyes matched his.

"Okay," he said, after a breath.

She was thrilled at her victory until he continued.

"If you're going to ignore all good sense and stay at your apartment, I'm sleeping on your sofa. End of story."

Satisfaction turned to outrage. "You most certainly are not."

"Zach," Noah said. "This isn't your call. You're off shift, and you've had a long day. Go home and rest."

Zach shot him a glance. "Is that an order since you're the chief now?"

"Interim chief," Noah said, putting his coffee mug down and wiping his mouth. "But don't make it that way." The cops glanced uneasily at each other. "You're putting in full-time hours. You're exhausted. This is Violet's call, not yours."

Violet's breath caught as the seconds ticked by. She could not stand to see tension between Zach and Noah, not now, not because of her. She touched his hand, just grazing his fingertips. "Zach," she murmured, then louder. "You win. I'll go to Mom and Dad's tomorrow, after I get some things together. I'm exhausted, and I want to tell the building's superintendent in the morning so I'll stay one more night at the apartment."

Her father frowned. "But tonight would be better, really, Vi..."

She gave him the sternest look she could manage. "I've made up my mind."

He huffed out a breath. "All right. Tomorrow morning. We'll get the room ready for you."

"By *we* he means me," her mother said.

"I'm not giving up my airport job, mind you, only my living space and only temporarily."

After another long moment Zach relaxed. It seemed as though all the cops in the room did, as well. "All right, but I'm still spending the night on your sofa," Zach said.

Her nerves ignited. “That sofa is as comfortable as sleeping on a sack of potatoes.”

“I’ll survive.”

“I don’t want you to bother.”

“No bother.”

“Zach, you can’t sleep on my sofa.” Exasperation crept into her tone.

“Then I’ll stretch out in your hallway and annoy the neighbors. They can step over me on the way to the elevator. The butcher will love it.”

She glared. He stared. She fisted her hands on her hips. He hooked thumbs in his utility belt and gave her a slow, sassy smile, one that said, “I win and there’s nothing you can do about it.” She could have resisted further, but the smile was edged with something deeper, something soft that played at the edges of his mouth, tangled with the stubbornness.

“The butcher stays awake until three in the morning and plays nonstop polka music,” she said in a last-ditch measure.

"Then I guess I'd better eat a hearty meal before I go off to the torture chamber." He had the audacity to wink at her.

She shook her head, biting back the retort that would not do any good, she realized.

"How about some lunch?" he said. "All these cops are starving, right, guys?"

They all broke into loud agreement, probably happy the standoff was at an end.

Zach cocked his head. "You see? Starving." He struck a plaintive expression that made him look all of ten years old. "Please feed us, Vi, before we keel over from hunger."

Violet looked from Zach to her parents, to all the other cops gathered around the table and she knew that she had lost the battle.

Fine, she resolved. *I'll do what you want, just for a while, but I'm not going to let good guys or bad guys have control over my life.*

"Lunch is coming right up," she said through gritted teeth.

FIVE

Violet whirled on her heel and marched to the kitchen. No need to ask orders of the assembled group; she'd bring them each their favorite sandwiches, which she'd memorized long ago, along with bowls of homemade soup, extra crackers on the side for Noah and a bagged chocolate chip cookie for Carter to take home to Ellie. Zach's favorite lunch was a pastrami on rye with extra spicy brown mustard, a glass of root beer, no ice, and a slice of apple pie, never à la mode. It was a meal he could devour with no guilt since he was a workout fiend and a star on the police basketball team. At least he had been known to devour all of that in one sitting before his brother was murdered.

Now more often than not he'd stick to coffee or pick at his food, asking her to wrap it up for later, but she doubted he'd eat it at all. He was thinner, his face a touch on the gaunt side. She missed seeing him power down a hearty meal and sigh in pleasure at her apple pie.

"Why does your pie taste better than anyone else's?" he would ask.

She'd never tell him the answer. She prepared every pie she made with painstaking care, because she imagined she was making them all for him. It had been that way since she was thirteen and he'd told her for the first time how much he enjoyed her pie.

Sappy, Vi. Get it together, girl.

If she couldn't salve his pain, she would follow the long-standing Griffin tradition of throwing food at the problem. *You're getting an extra-big piece of pie and you're going to eat it this time, buddy boy.*

As he took his customary place with his back to the wall, so he could track the comings and goings at the counter and front door, he kept his gaze on her every moment. Ignoring him and ladling up bowls of soup, she thought about what it would be like to have the brooding, determined Zach Jameson parked in her living room.

A year before, she'd been dating Otto, an NYPD detective. He was everything Zach wasn't: short and stocky, brilliant in math and languages, a lover of books and quiet walks. He was always there with a sweater to put around her shoulders or a bouquet of flowers to brighten her counter at Emerge. They'd had fun, but something was missing for both of them; that deep sense of "rightness" was the best way she could describe it.

They'd parted amicably, although part of her still wondered why she hadn't felt a deeper connection with Otto. He was an undeniably good man, though Zach had told her on more than one occasion he didn't think Otto was at all right for her.

You need somebody tougher, Vi, who can stand up to you, he'd said. *Somebody who can make you laugh.*

Somebody like himself? Of course, he hadn't meant that. So why exactly was Zach front and center in her thoughts at any given moment?

Natural, in light of what happened to his brother. Thoughts were okay; it was her heart that was off-limits since she had no intention of complicating her lifelong friendship with Zach. At least she was not prone to running into him on a daily basis, since she was at the airport forty hours a week. Keep busy, was her strategy; stay away from Zach, who awakened so many contradictory feelings she could not make heads nor tails of.

He was a family friend…yet, his blue eyes made her breath quicken.

He knew her better than anyone else in the world…yet, he shut her out at the worst moment in his life. He made her laugh like no one else on the planet, but the thought of him with another woman burned like acid.

Worst of all, she felt rattled and vulnerable after the attack, and the feelings were surfacing that she desperately did not want to share with a man who was increasingly making her weak in the knees.

So how exactly is having him under my roof going to work?

It was only for one night, she told herself. Better Zach sleeping on the sofa than her being alone with a drug dealer after her. The feel of Beck's fingers grabbing at her made her skin go clammy.

Silly. She was safe, completely so, within the walls of Griffin's Diner, surrounded by cops and dogs.

But what about when she returned to her airport job? Beck's threat came back to her.

A quick death is better. We could make it last much longer if we wanted to.

Suppressing a shiver, she loaded up her tray and delivered the food. She could tell at once that the tone had changed around the table. Zach was stiff-backed, jaw thrust forward.

"It wouldn't have made any difference whether you were there or not," K-9 officer Luke Hathaway said in response to something Violet hadn't heard. "Jenks would have bolted into traffic, anyway."

Violet knew that Claude Jenks was the man who had left the fake suicide note at the K-9 graduation ceremony that Jordy was to have facilitated. Jenks would have killed department secretary Sophie Walters, who'd discovered him in the act of leaving the note, if Luke hadn't intervened. Jenks had died denying he'd killed Jordan Jameson, before he could reveal the name of the murderer or the motive.

"Maybe not," Zach said. "Things might have gone differently if you had more help."

Luke's mouth hardened. "I was saving Sophie from drowning. You'd have done the same."

"I wasn't implying otherwise."

Luke's nostrils flared. "I think you were, Zach. Why don't you just spit it out? You want to blame me for Jenks's death, huh?"

Noah held up a calming hand. "No one is implying anything, Luke. Zach is just venting, and it's going to stop." He turned a hard stare on his brother. "We are not going to go after each other. It's bad enough with the reporters spreading the suicide theory all over. We're a unit and we'll stay that way. It's what Jordy would have wanted."

Zach jerked as though he'd been slapped. He pushed back his chair and stalked to the porch room, returning with Eddie. Violet stood frozen as he left the room and exited the restaurant.

Noah scrubbed a hand over his face and let out a long, weary breath. "Luke, don't hold it against him. He's hurting, and he doesn't know what to do about it." His look was pained as he sought Violet. "Vi, he will listen to you more than anyone. Do you think you can…?"

But she was already moving, praying God would give her the words to soothe Zach's tattered soul.

Zach leaned against the stone front of Griffin's, heart thundering in his chest.

It's what Jordy would have wanted... Noah was right. Jordy would never have tolerated him going at other members of the team, second-guessing their actions, heaping blame where it didn't belong. Shame squeezed his gut. *What's the matter with me?*

He looked at his boots when Violet approached. She stood with him, arms folded against the cold air.

"I know what you're going to say," he blurted. "Noah's right. I don't blame Luke. It wasn't his fault, it was mine. I should have been there, just like I should have sensed something was wrong, that someone was after Jordy. I should have..." He stopped abruptly as the pain closed off his throat. The back of his head banged against the hard stone behind him, and he closed his eyes. "I'm losing it."

And then she was embracing him, warm and soft, and his arms went around her as he buried his face in her neck.

"I was going to say it's okay," she whispered. "It's okay and I understand."

And with her there, he let himself hear it, clinging to her, willing her to say it again. His craving for comfort was so strong and it seemed like she was the only person who could give it to him. He didn't know how long he stayed like that, breathing in the scent of her hair, the fragrance of soup that clung to her clothes while she murmured gentle, soothing things against his cheek.

This isn't your fault.

I'm praying for you.

Praying. Lifting him up to a God whom he despised. He did not know if he could stand it, but nevertheless he grasped at the words, feeling the steady beat of her heart that somehow made his own keep on pulsing in spite of the pain that nearly crippled him. She felt like a life preserver in his arms, holding him just above the water that was trying so hard to pull him under. He wanted to lose himself in her embrace.

"I'm sorry," he mumbled against her neck. "You shouldn't have to prop me up after what you've been through today."

She pulled him away then, and put her hands on his face, stroking thumbs over his cheeks. Her eyes brimmed with emotion and strength.

"I will always be here for you, Zach, always." She kissed him where she could reach, aiming for his cheek and getting the corner of his mouth instead. Prickles formed all over and everything in him wanted to bend and capture her mouth to his properly. The thought startled him.

What are you doing? This is Violet, re-

member? A longtime family friend who's just being nice because you're a complete basket case. For a moment he was paralyzed between the logic of his head and the needs of his heart. Warmth, comfort, soothing, friends, duty, honor…love?

Let her go.

With effort, he finally released her. Her cheeks were pink, probably from her work in the diner, or the cold, and a single long curl that had escaped the barrette grazed the side of her face. He used one finger to pull it away from the satin curve of her cheekbone.

"I do not deserve a friend like you," he said.

Something glimmered in those brown irises. Another few seconds and she smoothed her apron and sent him a saucy grin. "You're right. You don't."

That was the Violet he knew. Strong and sassy. A die-hard friend who would not bring up his moment of embarrassing weakness again. He sighed, cleared his throat, called to Eddie and they reentered the diner. He wasn't hungry, but he knew he'd get grief for not eating, so he made a stab at it. Noah and the others were eating, too. He waited until some of the team had gotten up to go before he caught Luke's attention.

"Sorry, man," he said. "You did the right thing. I was just blowing off some steam, but I shouldn't have directed it at you. There's no excuse for what I said."

Luke shrugged. "I get it. We're gonna figure out what happened to Jordy and someone is going to pay for it."

Carter and Noah nodded. "Copy that," Carter said.

His gaze drifted to Violet, who was cleaning up after the lunch service. For a moment he remembered the feel of her misplaced kiss, the silken caress of her wandering curl. He blinked back to reality. Jordy's case was still digging at him, but now he had another matter to attend to: keeping her safe and putting Xavier Beck behind bars.

He noticed Violet's curl, the one he'd touched, was loose again, a ribbon of brown silk against her cheek. His stomach tightened when he remembered his urge to kiss her. She did indeed represent all the things he craved…warmth, comfort, friendship, duty, honor…but love? No. Violet Griffin wasn't meant to be that for him.

No more confusion, Zach.

You have a job to do.

Don't mess this one up.

SIX

After she'd cleaned up from the dinner hour and left the kitchen spotless, Violet found Zach and Eddie waiting outside the diner. Zach drove to Violet's apartment. The more she fumed, the more cheerful he became, an annoying strategy he'd learned early on in their relationship.

"Don't mind us," Zach said, plopping down on her sofa and flipping on the TV to the sports channel. Eddie wasted no time scrambling up next to him, since he wasn't allowed on the sofa at their home. "We've stayed in much worse accommodations. We'll just catch some sports news and fix ourselves a snack later. Pretend like we aren't even here."

Like that was possible. Violet shut the bathroom door more forcefully than was strictly necessary, stripped off her soiled work uniform and showered until the hot water ran out. Marginally restored, she slid into a pair of comfortable jeans and a soft sweater. It was still only a little after eight, and the evening stretched in awkward hours before her. What was she supposed to do with Zach sitting out there?

Zach still lounged on her couch, legs sprawled out in front of him. Eddie curled up at his hip. Eddie wasn't exactly the ferocious, killer K-9. More of a lovable couch potato, she thought fondly, certainly much more easygoing than his owner.

Since she'd been too busy to eat dinner, she cooked grilled cheese and warmed up some soup for a late meal. Without asking, she set Zach a place at the table, too, happy to see him dig in with gusto. Why was it so satisfying to feed this man? Sure, she'd enjoyed preparing her best dishes for Otto, but there was something so downright fulfilling about feeding Zach Jameson. It mystified her.

"No people food for Eddie," he called, catching her in the act of treating Eddie to a leftover crust of bread.

"Says the man who bakes gourmet treats for his dog."

"Like I tell my brothers when they rag on me about it, Eddie works hard. He deserves quality rewards. I make them out of approved organic ingredients and besides, it's the only thing I know how to cook. If there really is a zombie apocalypse, Eddie and I are going to survive on gourmet dog treats and if you are very nice, we will share with you."

She laughed, enjoying the friendly teasing, the comfort of a shared meal. Remembering the peanut butter cookies she'd stowed in the freezer, she was about to try and tempt him with dessert, but he excused himself to take a call. When he returned, a frown etched his brow.

"We pulled the info for the Emerge Airline frequent fliers in the past six months. Beck showed up, Roach twice and one more guy. Do you recognize him?" He showed her a picture on his phone.

Her stomach clenched. "Yes. I've seen him several times. Is he connected with Beck and Roach?"

"Probably, but he's likely just a small-time courier. Last time they all flew to Miami. Their destinations were different this time. One was headed to Miami, and Roach to San Francisco. This third guy, Victor Jones, has got a record, but no outstanding warrants at the moment. We'll find him and ask some questions, but it's best that..."

"Don't even say it. I'm going back to work tomorrow."

He scowled. "I don't like it."

"You'll have to live with it."

He rapped his knuckles on the table. "How come you get to be irrationally stubborn and I don't?"

"Woman's prerogative," she said.

He sighed and said little for the rest of the evening.

She tried to watch her favorite home decorating show on TV, but Zach's restlessness prevented her from sticking with it. He would stroll to the window periodically and look down onto the darkened street. Then it would be back to his phone, checking messages, and several times he completed a series of pushups on the kitchen floor. Eddie's brows twitched as he took it all in from the comfort of the sofa.

"How can you stand it?" she asked the dog. "Doesn't he ever sit still?"

Eddie blew out a breath, ruffling his lips.

When Zach started in on arranging her shelf of cookbooks for the second time, she abandoned her magazine. "Zach, you're driving me bonkers."

His brows shot up in surprise. "I am?"

"Yes. Can't you relax for a couple of minutes?"

He blinked as if taking internal inventory. "I am relaxed."

"I'm sorry to be the one to break this to you, but no, you're not anywhere close to relaxed. You're like an overwound top."

"Oh. Is it the pacing?"

"The pacing, pushups, rearranging and the like. I'm afraid you're going to start busting out walls and remodeling my apartment when you run out of other things to do."

"Yeah, okay, sorry. Carter says the same thing only he doesn't use such nice words. How about I go take a shower? Sometimes that will do the trick."

"An excellent idea," she said. "Use all the hot water you want. Please."

"Yeah, Carter says that, too." Chuckling, he disappeared into the tiny bathroom.

She smiled to herself. Zach had always been like a fully wound clock, forever in motion, driven by some internal engine. At times it got on her very last nerve, but the moments when he was still and thoughtful and fully attentive were precious as pure sunlight. Violet was just settling in to her magazine when her phone buzzed with a text.

It's Nan. I'm downstairs. Purse stolen so I'm borrowing this phone. Buzz me in?

Textbook Nan. The girl in apartment 315 would probably lose her head if it wasn't fastened securely. It was a wonder to Violet how her friend kept her job as a receptionist in a dental office.

Violet texted back.

Buzzing you in.

She buzzed and opened her magazine again.

Not working, Nan texted a few minutes later.

Violet sighed. Door problems were a common occurrence in her aging apartment complex. She slipped on her animal-print flats and let herself out without disturb-

ing Eddie, who still had eyes locked on the bathroom door, waiting for Zach to emerge.

She took the elevator down to the lobby. Through the lobby doors, she saw a car parked on the curb, probably the Uber Nan had taken. Violet did not intend to do anything stupid, considering her own precarious situation. Unless she saw her friend Nan through the glass panel of the front lobby door, she had no intention of opening it. She had not made it two steps away from the elevator when the stairwell door opened. In a matter of moments Xavier Beck had pulled her in, the door closing behind them.

She tried to scream, but he clamped a calloused hand over her mouth and jerked her tightly to his shoulder. “Hello, Violet.”

He smelled of cigarettes. His stubbled chin rasped against her face. “Thought you’d ditched me for good? It was easy to wait and sneak into the building behind some oblivious tenant. Her name tag read

'Nan.' She looked about your age, so I took a chance that you knew her. I didn't think you'd actually fall for the *buzzer didn't work* trick. Dumber than you look."

Fear nearly left her immobile, but she kicked, her shoe coming loose, missing her target. There was a camera in the stairwell at the first landing, but they were not quite in view of it. Beck must have known because he pulled her in the other direction, backing into the panic bar of the basement door.

The basement…no cameras, no help, no way for Zach to know how to find her. Now she felt the full onslaught of panic, kicking and twisting, trying to scream as Beck dragged her down the flight of stairs, pushing open the heavy door with his boot.

He shoved her inside and she fell to one knee, but only for a moment as she scrambled to get away. Beck flicked on the bare hanging bulb, which illuminated the space

in a ghastly glow. The smell of mildew mixed with the sharp odor of bleach.

A labyrinth of tall shelves stretched from cement floor to dripping ceiling, cluttered with bottles and tools, plastic containers that looked as though they hadn't been opened in decades, a moldering fake Christmas tree lying like a corpse across a shelf. The opposite wall housed a set of washing machines and dryers. She jerked backward as far as she could go until her shoulders banged into a washing machine behind her.

Beck's expression was relaxed, happy, almost, as he shut the basement door, wedging a doorstop under it. "Don't you want to scream? No one would hear you, anyway, but it would make this game more fun."

She clamped her chattering teeth together. She would never give him the satisfaction. "They'll find you. They'll arrest you," she said.

"The cops?" He laughed. "You know who wins in the end, at this game of life, I mean?

The ones who don't follow the rules. Cops have to follow the rules. Me? I haven't followed any rules since I was twelve years old. Cops always lose."

She tried another tack. "I… I won't testify. I'll forget what I saw in your suitcase."

"Oh, I'm sure you wouldn't, but you don't get to the top in this business by leaving loose ends. I'm going to prove to my boss that I'm ready for bigger responsibilities." He grinned. "Your death will be a line item on my résumé." He pulled a knife from his pocket. The tip of it shone white in the dim glow. "Ready?"

Zach felt it as soon as he exited the bathroom. Violet was gone. He sprinted to her room to confirm that she was not there. He couldn't wrap his mind around it. What could have persuaded her to leave the safety of the apartment? To leave his protection? He yanked open the apartment door, but there was no sign of her in the hall.

Trying to still his rattling nerves, he shoved his gun into the waistband of his jeans and shut Eddie in the apartment with a stern admonishment. "Don't chew anything up." Then he was jogging to the elevator. He gave the button a half dozen pushes and waited for an interminable amount of time before he decided to take the stairs.

Everything was fine, he told himself. There had to be a good outcome here. No need to freak out, but his legs churned faster and faster until he reached the first floor. Sprinting into the lobby, he found the super strolling by the mailboxes, a screwdriver sticking out of his plaid pocket.

"Where's Violet Griffin?" he demanded.

"How should I know that? The tenants don't have to show me hall passes or anything." His narrow mustache quivered as he laughed at his own joke.

Zach ground his teeth. "Did you see her come down here recently?"

"No. I just came a second ago to unjam a

mailbox." He squinted at Zach. "What are you doing here, by the way? You're a cop, right? The one with the dog? I've seen you in uniform before. Is there a problem?"

Oh, yeah. Big problem. His stomach clenched into a fist. Where was she? "When you came down did you take the elevator or the stairs?"

"The elevator, and it was just me, if that's your next question."

"Go look at the lobby camera footage right now. Tell me if you see where she was headed and if anyone was with her. Text me."

"What's your…?"

Zach grabbed a pen from the manager's pocket and before he could protest, Zach scrawled his cell number on the man's palm. "Do it. Now."

He left the manager gaping, texted Noah and dashed out to the sidewalk, holding open the door with a chair so he wouldn't get locked out. There was no sign of her in the bitter cold. The damp sidewalk sent shock waves through his bare feet since he'd not taken the time to put on his shoes. Doubling back he reentered the stairwell. Nothing on the landing.

He looked again and his breath caught.

A woman's shoe, Violet's animal-print flat. He put himself in the assailant's mind. He'd waited patiently until a resident had shown up and snuck into the building when they buzzed the door open. Concocting some story, he'd gotten Violet to come down, giving her an excuse she'd believed.

There was a lobby camera, but it was facing the outer doors and didn't catch the stairwell action or maybe the guy didn't care. Had they taken her out of the building via the front entrance? He didn't think they'd risk it since someone on the street might have seen them and she'd be struggling for all she was worth. Back upstairs? Why? The answer sickened him. To find a secluded place to kill her, a place where her screams would not be heard.

His phone signaled a text from the manager.

Short, muscled guy pulled her into the stairwell. Don't know if they were going up or down.

His heart slammed his ribs. Up or down? Upstairs, ignoring the cameras? Pulling an unwilling victim? No, Zach thought. He'd go down—easier, closer—to the basement laundry room. He swallowed. Soundproof.

Terror filled him as he considered. Beck would likely kill her in the basement where they wouldn't be interrupted, where it would be hours or more before anyone discovered her.

The manager texted again.

What can I do?

Cops are on their way. Go open the lobby

doors. Then lock yourself in your office and wait for them to arrive.

But...

Do it.

He heaved at the basement door and found it jammed. Kicking with all the strength he could bring to bear, he succeeded in forcing it open. The wedge of wood that had secured it skidded across the floor, lost in the darkness. Dropping as low as he could, gun drawn, he made entry.

Dank air assaulted his senses as he took up a position behind a tower of crates and listened.

Voices?

A woman's, high and scared. Violet.

"Police!" Zach shouted at the top of his lungs. "Let her go."

The answer came in a scream. “Zach, he’s got a knife.”

“Hold on, Violet, I’m coming!” he yelled before he charged.

SEVEN

Violet could not breathe through the fear that clawed at her chest. Zach would be an easy target for Beck's knife. What could she do?

"Drop your weapon!" Zach shouted again.

She could not figure out where Beck had gotten to until she heard the creak of protesting metal. He was behind a shelving unit, circling around Zach, who could not possibly spot him in the insufficient light.

She could only think of one thing to do. She grabbed up the first item her hands could reach, an old toolbox that was almost rusted through. Flinging the top open, she began throwing the contents as fast and as hard as she could in Beck's direction. An old screwdriver, a file, a series of clamps and finally the toolbox itself. The heavy metal container crashed with a thunderous noise into the spot where she figured Beck was waiting, clipping the overhead light, shattering the lightbulb and plunging the room into complete darkness. The ink-black compounded her terror. Any moment she expected to feel a knife plunging into her back or hear Zach fall victim to Beck's ambush.

She fumbled for her phone to turn on the flashlight. The clang of metal and crash of something falling nearby almost made her scream. Was it Beck running? Going after Zach? Coming around for her again? Glass crunched only a few feet away. Finally, her shaking fingers found the light button and she was about to flick it on, until a hand reached out from the gloom.

Another hand wrapped around her mouth from behind, muffling the scream that was erupting from her lips.

"Shhhh," Zach whispered in her ear. "It's me. No light. I don't want him to see you."

Her knees went weak with relief as he released her and kept her close. His body was wire taut. He put his mouth near and spoke in her ear. "Get out, well away from here, and text my brothers with your location. They should be here any minute. I'm going to find him. He has to be in the basement still unless there's an easy exit where he wouldn't be spotted leaving."

She clutched at his forearm. "No. He'll kill you."

He pushed her firmly away a step. "Gonna get him, Vi. Do what I say. Now."

Fear flashed through her. *Cops always lose.* "Please, Zach. No."

"You're not giving orders here."

"Zach..."

This time he didn't answer, just dropped a kiss on her temple and propelled her to the threshold so fast she almost stumbled.

When she turned around again, he was gone, vanishing into the shadows.

Her blood turned to ice, and a wave of fear overwhelmed her, for a moment she could not move. Beck's words assaulted her again.

You know who wins in the end...?

Zach would play by the rules—he already had, by identifying himself as a cop, making himself a target. Beck would kill Zach without a second thought.

Her fingernails cut into her palms. Desperate to run to Zach, she had to do what he said, or risk making the problem worse. *Text the Jamesons.* Stumbling over the threshold, she raced into the hallway and frantically texted Noah, but the message failed to send, thanks to her position deep in the building. She took the stairs two at a time, panic driving her. Almost at the exit to the lobby she yelped as a German shepherd dog lunged at her, barking viciously.

Carter pulled Frosty back with a sharp command. “Are you hurt?”

“No. Zach’s in the basement with Beck. Beck’s got a knife.”

“We got his text. Keep going until you’re out of here.” Carter barreled by her, Frosty rigid with excitement. She continued her mindless sprint, emerging into the lobby where she found Luke Hathaway and his German shepherd, Bruno.

Luke guided her to a corner of the lobby away from the swarm of patrol cops. Noah Jameson was there, speaking into his radio. He gave her a nod, but he did not approach her. The intensity on his face aged him. She could not conceive of how he could do his job when another of his brothers could possibly lose his life at any moment. How could he calmly work the scene while Zach was in the basement with a lunatic?

Save him, she wanted to scream. *You’ve got to save him.*

But that was exactly what Noah and the

assembled officers were trying to do, she re-alized. As much as she wanted to run right back down to that basement, she would do as instructed and not become another prob-lem for the cops to deal with.

In control, strong, like she always was, but in truth, her legs felt like wet noodles. The whole thing was her fault. How could she have been so stupid to deliver herself to the lobby for Beck to abduct?

The building's super appeared at her elbow. "Zach told me to lock myself in the office until I saw the cops. Uh, er, are you okay? You're missing a shoe, and you look terrible. Did they catch the guy yet?"

Violet forced a steadying breath and gave the super a stripped-down account of what had transpired.

He shook his head. "And the worst thing I had to deal with today was a stopped-up toilet and a jammed mailbox."

Violet could not manage a reply, but she was relieved that the super went to talk to the other tenants who had begun to assemble in the lobby. The patrol cop in charge told them in no uncertain terms to clear the area but they were slow in dispersing, curious to know why there was a one-shoed tenant on the verge of hysteria holding up a wall of the building. Each breath was an effort. Would the door open to Carter's mournful face if he could not save yet another brother?

All she could do was stand there like a statue, praying like crazy that God would keep Zach safe.

A cop jogged in from outside. "Spotted Beck running as I pulled up. I pursued on foot but I lost him. He…"

"He was too quick for me, too," Zach said as he followed the cop in.

Violet's heart nearly jumped from her chest at the sight of him. It was all she could do to keep her tears from flowing and fight the urge to throw her arms around him and squeeze the breath from his lungs.

"Carter's checking the nearby shops, but I think Beck had a vehicle somewhere close by." Zach conferred with his colleagues for a moment while Violet simply stared and willed her legs to hold her up. She hunched over, trying to draw in steadying breaths. Zach came to her side.

"Hey. You okay?"

She nodded, still not looking at him. He crooked a finger under her chin and tipped her head up.

"Serious?"

"Yes," she said through chattering teeth. She wanted him to stay there, holding her arms, telling her he was all right, that the whole crazy situation was going to be okay, but she could make no sound at all.

"You lost a shoe," he said, holding her hand.

"A good excuse to get new ones."

He smiled. "Since when do you need an excuse? You've got more shoes than Bloomingdale's."

"At least I'm wearing one. You're barefoot." Violet wanted to fire back another sassy remark. Instead, she put her head on his chest to hide her face.

"You… I…when you went after him… I was…scared."

He stroked her hair. "I'm sorry you were scared, but that's my job, Vi, and I'm gonna do it, especially if it means making sure you're safe."

Safe. She wondered if she would ever feel safe again.

"I shouldn't have gone down to the lobby. It was dumb."

He bent down to look at her, his expression stern. "This isn't your fault. None of it. You're not gonna feel that way, hear me?"

Some of her load of misery lifted. She wanted to fall into his blue eyes and float there in a sea of azure, far away from the current madness.

He tucked her into the crook of his arm. "I don't think he'll be back, but just in case,

I'm taking you to your parents' house to-night and I'm sure you aren't going to argue with me this time."

"Okay," Violet said.

Zach frowned. "Okay? No arguments?"

"Uh-uh." Violet bent, both to take off her remaining shoe and conceal her fear. "You're right. I'll go. I should have listened to you in the first place."

He squeezed her around her shoulders. "I wish I could get that last bit on tape. That's not your typical comeback."

She tried for bravado. "It hasn't been a typical night. I… I mean, he could've…" The feel of Beck's arm locked around her throat shook her again. Tears gathered in her eyes, to her dismay, and she gulped them back.

Zach pulled her a bit closer and walked her to the elevator, calling over his shoulder, "Taking her upstairs to pack a bag. Be down in five."

Noah nodded, still talking to a group of officers clustered around him.

When the elevator doors closed, Zach took her in his arms. "I'm sorry this happened, Vi." He tucked her underneath his chin, his breath warm on her hair. "You don't deserve any of this."

She crushed herself to his chest and stayed there, breathing, trying to control the rampant flood of emotions. Xavier Beck's threats rang loud and clear in her ears. But she had to be strong, she told herself, calm and in control, like he expected. *Zach needs you to keep it together.*

"You know, it's…okay not to be okay," he said into her hair. "Talk about it if you need to."

It hit her like a slap. Was he really saying that she should be vulnerable with him? Asking her to spill her guts? Her self-control started to erode. She jerked away from him. "So it's fine for me to express my inner angst but not you?"

He looked startled. "Well, I mean, it's healthy to talk about it, right? That's what everybody says after a traumatic incident."

"For me, you mean, but not for a tough K-9 cop."

He offered a smile. "Right, well, that goes without saying, doesn't it?"

"No, it doesn't."

He shifted uneasily. "I don't understand why I'm in trouble here."

She goggled at him. "You can't keep your feelings locked away in a vault and expect me to share mine."

He didn't answer, just scrubbed a palm over his face. "Where is this coming from? It's kind of out of the blue."

"It most certainly is not. It's been coming on since your brother was killed."

He flinched, but she pressed on. "It's okay that you're struggling with Jordy's death, Zach, and like you said, it's healthy to talk about it."

He did not meet her eye, but his mouth

hardened into a firm line. "I don't need to talk about it. I'm dealing, Vi."

"No, you're not. You're angry and blaming God and it's making you nuts that you can't solve your own brother's murder."

He folded his arms across his chest, staring at the mirrored doors, tone hard and flat. "This isn't the time."

"Yes, it is. If you want me to share my feelings, then you can share yours."

His twitching jaw muscle told her what he thought of that idea. Without looking at her he said, "I…just want you to be all right. I'm sorry if I offended you."

Silence spooled out between them as she regarded Zach in the steel doors. So tall, strong, macho, but with his bare feet and the bemused expression and the pain that he was trying so desperately to keep sealed away, she saw his truest self: a man hurting, her best friend, whom she could have easily lost forever. She felt the anger drain out of her.

"You didn't offend me." He would not meet her eye. "And I want the same for you, Zach. I want to help you be all right, if you'll let me." Had her words been too plaintive? Too pushy? Too laced with longing that she hadn't hidden away properly?

The silence went on for a beat longer. "Why don't we talk about something else… like your baseball skills? Taking out the lights with a screwdriver, I didn't know you had it in you." His laugh was forced, tense, but the message was clear.

I don't want this.

She was changing the rules of their relationship and he wasn't ready or willing to do so. What did he want from her? Strength, wit, friendship, nothing more, nothing deeper.

Her spirit sagged. So be it. Those were the things she would give him, then. Nothing more, nothing deeper. Swallowing hard, she watched the buttons count off the floors one by one.

The silence was deafening by the time the elevator finally delivered them back to her apartment. She unlocked the door and gasped. Zach immediately pushed ahead of her, took in the surroundings and groaned. The sofa sported an eight-inch hole in the cushion, the stuffing spilling out onto the floor. Eddie was nowhere in sight.

"Officer Eddie, get your sorry self in here right now," Zach thundered.

The dog slunk from behind the couch, his face more hound dog at that moment than beagle. "What do you have to say for yourself? You're supposed to be a highly trained police K-9."

Eddie offered a half-hearted wag of his tail and a yip at his master. A bit of stuffing clung to his whiskers.

"Don't you try to make nice with me, dog. You ruined Violet's sofa. I hope you thoroughly enjoyed yourself, because you are in deep trouble. This will be reflected in your service record."

Eddie whined, ears down and then let loose with a pitiful baying.

Violet could not help the laughter that bubbled up from her mouth. Whether it was born of relief, or trauma, the giggles escalated until tears ran down her face and she doubled over.

"I'm glad you find this amusing," Zach said, glowering at her and the dog. "Now I gotta pay for a couch."

She could not restrain another peal of laughter. "At least you don't have to worry about sleeping on it."

A hint of a smile quirked his mouth and he let out a world-weary sigh. "Go pack your bag, Vi. Officer Chewsalot and I need to have a talk about behavior and life choices and the extent of his grounding."

"Yes, sir," Violet said, still giggling as she went to fetch her suitcase. *Maybe you can get the dog to open up about his feelings*, she thought, giving Eddie a little pat as she walked out.

EIGHT

Zach gave Violet an encouraging nod as she held the phone between them in the front seat of his Tahoe, dialed Bill Oscar and clicked on the speakerphone. He'd cautioned her vigorously not to mention anything about what had transpired at her apartment building. Bill might have orchestrated the whole attack, after all, and there was still a chance a cop might apprehend Beck before the night was over.

"I'm sorry for the late notice, Bill, but I am going to take your advice and not come in tomorrow. My mom really needs help with the puppy and..." She swallowed. "I'm not feeling at the top of my game, to be honest."

As close as Violet would come to admitting she was rattled. "Good job," he mouthed.

"No problem, Vi," Bill said. "I understand completely. It's about time you started to use up that mountain of vacation time you have on the books."

She thanked him again and disconnected.

Zach had listened intently and did not hear any indication of suspicion in Bill's voice. Either the guy was a great actor or he believed Violet's excuse. It gave him some breathing room as he escorted Violet to the front door of her parents' home.

She paused on the doorstep. The light of the streetlamp painted her in an ethereal glow, like a portrait he'd seen of a woman looking down at her moonlit garden. Was it the light that made her look so delicate or perhaps had his vision changed since he'd come so close to losing her in that basement?

His breathing hitched. He wanted to put his arms around her, to feel her warm breath on his neck, to reassure her and himself. But he was still confused by what had happened earlier between them in the elevator.

If you want me to share my feelings, then you can share yours.

Was that what he wanted? That mutual sharing of the deepest parts of themselves? But that was more than friendship, wasn't it?

"Good night, Zach." As she opened the door he saw Lou hastening toward her. Zach stepped away, wiggled his fingers at her and left her to the comfort of her worried father.

He was satisfied as he and Eddie returned home that at least Violet would be safe for one day and he'd have another chance to convince her to stop working for Bill Oscar, just until he figured out if Bill was guilty or not. It wasn't like he was trying to force her to give up her career or anything.

Lying in bed, he stared at the ceiling. Though his body ached from exhaustion, his mind would not allow him to sleep. The moment in the elevator kept poking at him. What did Violet want him to do, flop down on her ruined sofa and share all of his innermost feelings with her? That wasn't the kind of relationship they had. They were friends, jovial, supportive, yes, but upbeat always. Violet was a tough lady, sure of herself and ready with a wisecrack, just like she'd always been. He couldn't imagine where she'd come up with the notion that they should cry on each other's shoulders. Then again, he'd practically cried on hers outside the diner, and for some reason it hadn't felt awkward at all.

More and more he found himself puzzling and worrying over what Violet Griffin might be thinking and yes, every so often, he felt the urge to unburden himself to her about the ravenous wolf gnawing away at his insides, the case he could not solve, the brother who was lost to him forever. There were others, a long line of people from brothers to his parents, buddies and even a cop shrink, who would listen to an emotional rant from Zach Jameson, so why could he only imagine sharing with Violet and no one else? Familiarity, it had to be. He'd known her forever.

He pictured Violet's mocha eyes and the sassy curve of her mouth, and in his mind she looked as she had on the doorstep, more tender and less tough, more wounded than wisecracking. There went the hitch in his breath again when he thought of her. He was losing it, pure and simple.

Aww, go to sleep, already, wouldja? Resolved to push Violet and everything else from his brain, he yanked up the covers and rolled onto his stomach.

After a night of fitful rest at best, he got up at dawn, pulled on a NYPD sweat suit and went out for a run in the chilly predawn of Thursday morning. Eddie, though a fairly energetic dog, was not the "jog four miles" type of animal, so he left him sleeping off his antics from the night before. Zach could only hope he had not ingested any of the sofa stuffing he'd worked so hard to disgorge. He ran long and hard, setting a pace that would drive away the angst and clear his confusion. Sweating and more relaxed, he returned to the kitchen he shared with his brothers, their families and his mom and dad, to find his six-year-old niece Ellie waiting for him.

"Hey, squirt."

"Hiya, Uncle Zach. Ready?"

"For what?"

"You forgot." Her cornflower eyes looked at him accusatorially. He scanned the counter and saw the ingredients she'd laid out: natural peanut butter, honey, wheat flour.

"No, I didn't."

"Yes, he did," Violet said, entering. "Before you lecture, an officer walked me over from next door." Her hair was caught into a loose ponytail, and she wore a shirt with greens and golds that coaxed the color of autumn leaves from her eyes. At that moment it hit him that Violet was insanely beautiful. It must have been some sort of profound idiocy that he had never noticed it before. He dropped the kitchen towel.

"No, squirt," Zach said, hastily grabbing it up again. "I remembered that it's dog-treat baking day." He grabbed a ceramic bowl and began to crack eggs into it. "Eddie's down to his last dozen or so."

The little girl nodded solemnly. "And I marked it on the calendar. See?" She pointed to a little dog bone drawn in brown marker. "That means baking day."

"Right," Zach said, whisking the eggs and slopping some over the side in the process. "Baking day, and I've got the best helper in the world. And you work cheap, too."

"One dollar," she said, but she looked troubled.

"Whatsa matter, squirt?"

Ellie squinched up her button nose and

sent a sidelong glance at Violet. “Violet knows how to cook more things than I do. Maybe she should be your helper.”

“No way, Ellie. I only know how to make people things, not dog things,” Violet said. “I’m just here to bring over some muffins, anyway.” Violet kissed Ellie. He looked for signs that she was overtired, stressed from the trauma she’d endured, but she seemed in perfect control as always. “I’m heading to the diner.” She held up a palm. “Carter’s taking me. You two enjoy treat-baking day.”

“I want to talk to you, Vi,” Zach said.

“Later. Dog treats take top priority.” She gave Ellie a thumbs-up and left.

Ellie watched her go. “I like Violet.”

“I like her, too, even if she does argue with me.”

“Why don’t you marry her, then?”

He dropped an egg onto the floor. Before he could grab the paper towels, she got the salt and sprinkled it onto the smashed egg, scooping it up easily.

“Where’d you learn that trick?”

“From Violet. So why don’t you marry her? She’s pretty and friendly and she knows how to cook and take care of dogs and people.”

He cracked another egg and got it into the bowl this time. “’Cause we’re just friends. Friends don’t get married.”

“Daddy said Mommy was his best friend before she died.”

That one stopped him. What was the best way to answer? Distraction, he remembered. Carter always tried that when Ellie was fixated on something. “I…uh…do you want to mix?”

“No. Mixing is your job. You have bigger muscles.”

“But my muscles are tired.”

She tipped her head, solemnly considering in that way that made him turn to mush.

“I am the roller and the cutter,” she said. “I don’t do the mixing. Do you want me to get Uncle Noah to help since your muscles are tired?"

He chuckled. "I think I have enough energy to mix."

"Good. I have to do the other parts." Ellie was the one who had helped him find the dog treat recipe in the first place, sitting with him to pore over pet cookbooks, testing out several recipes until they found the perfect palate pleaser for Eddie. Ellie was great at reminding him about the next step when he forgot, and patiently setting the timer when he tried to impress her by saying he didn't need to set one. Wise beyond her years, tender and sweet, and he was proud to be her uncle. And he'd be one to Katie and Jordy's child, too, the best uncle he could possibly be. Swallowing back a tide of bittersweet emotion, he set to work.

When the dough was mixed, she rolled it out, pressing the tiny bone cookie cutter into the brown goo and loading the shapes onto the cookie trays.

"How hot do I set the…?"

"Four hundred twenty-five," she said. "For…"

"Ten minutes," he said. "I remembered that one."

"That's great. You're doing a good job, Uncle Zach."

He laughed. "Thanks. I haven't had to use the fire extinguisher in a long time, have I?"

"That's because we set the timer."

He tugged at her ponytail. "What would I do without you?"

"You would have to pay someone else a dollar to help you. Like Violet. She would help you even without the dollar."

Zach tried to forestall any more marriage suggestions by washing up the bowls and sliding the pan of baked treats out of the oven. They passed a happy half hour until Noah came in and poured coffee.

"Good morning, squirt," he said, kissing her cheek. "Your daddy said to remind you to brush your teeth."

"Can I do it later?"

Noah pretended to consider before he shook his head. "Your teeth will be sad if you wait."

"I don't think teeth get sad."

"But your daddy does, so go do it now, okay?"

"Okay." Ellie trotted off.

Noah looked at the coffeepot. "Did you make it?"

"No, Carter did."

"Excellent, then I'll have some." Noah poured himself a cup.

Zach ignored the jibe and washed the dishes. "Vi settled?"

"Yeah. All quiet at the diner. Carter made sure there's a detective outside." He fetched a water bottle and twisted off the top. "Got a tip on Victor Jones."

The third man frequenting Bill Oscar's ticket counter at Emerge Airlines. Zach perked up. "Yeah?"

"Snitch we popped says Jones hangs out

at a bagel shop in Pomonok, selling drugs when he can, mostly on Thursdays, though he's been away from it for a while. We're staking it out today. I'm not even going to ask if you want in."

"Waste of breath," Zach said, sprinting for the stairs. He was showered, changed into street clothes and had Eddie secured in a civilian leash and harness by the time Noah finished his cup of coffee.

"Scotty will be sorry he's missing out," Zach said, eyeing the rottweiler's police leash hanging on a hook.

"Especially since he hates having his teeth cleaned, but I promised him a cheeseburger when I pick him up tonight." Noah paused. "I stopped in to see Katie yesterday afternoon."

His heart thunked with pain at the mention of Jordy's widow. "How's she doing? Baby okay?"

"Baby is healthy, though the doctor is concerned Katie isn't gaining enough weight.

She isn't sleeping, but Sophie is plying Katie with food all the time and checking on her daily, like everybody else." Noah cleared his throat. "Katie says she keeps having dreams where Jordan and Snapper walk through the door."

A painful reminder of what she'd lost, what they'd all lost. Zach exhaled against the anguish. "Any new word on Snapper?"

"Couple more possible sightings. After the news first broke, people thought they saw German shepherds all over Queens, but nothing's panned out."

The more time that passed, the worse chance they had of finding Snapper alive. It was possible, maybe probable, that Jordy's abductor had killed the dog, too. It wouldn't have been easy. Snapper would have fought to the death to defend Jordy. He remembered working a parade with his older brother when a guy high on drugs took a swing at Jordy. The guy had been so scared of the barking and snapping teeth he'd begged to be taken to jail.

If you're out there, Snapper, hang on, buddy. We'll find you.

Zach finished the water and slammed the bottle into the trash. There had to be something, some bit of hope in the midst of this disaster. Arresting Victor Jones might just get them some info on who was running the airport smuggling operation. Bill Oscar? The shadowy Uno?

Noah put his cup down, interrupting Zach's thoughts. "Katie said she's praying that we are all dealing with this okay."

"Praying? She can save her breath. God's not answering." He grabbed his cell phone and jammed it into his pocket.

"Yes, He is," Noah said, voice low. "We just can't hear Him right now, but we'll feel His comfort in time."

God doesn't care, he wanted to tell his brother, but he could not say such a thing, not in the house where his parents had raised them to be men of faith; not in the place Jordy would have taken him to task for railing at God.

It occurred to Zach that his brother looked tired, haggard, as if the weight of the universe rested on his shoulders. How was Noah managing to deal with his own grief and lead the K-9 unit in that calm and reasoned way of his? No blowups or angry venting from Noah. Zach admired his brother, his skills, his quiet strength and his faith. He blew out a breath. Maybe he would pray again someday, but it wouldn't be today.

They loaded up in their Chevy Tahoes and took off for the bagel shop. As he drove away he peeked at the top floor of the Griffin household, which was dark, of course, because the whole family was busy at work serving breakfast at the diner, which was a scant fifteen minutes from the Jameson home. Hopefully, Violet would stay put, but there was a needy puppy to be dealt with, so she'd probably be going back and forth. There would be a cop assigned to watch her and he felt infinitely better knowing that during her puppy care stints, she was right next door to a houseful of cops and dogs, depending on the hour, instead of alone in her apartment.

Traffic was no worse than usual, and they made it in less than a half hour. Noah took up a position in his car, away from the store. It would not be unusual to see a cop car parked along a busy city block. Zach had to prowl around for fifteen minutes before he finally found a spot vacated by a departing delivery truck. He began to unobtrusively stroll the street, his earpiece hidden beneath a Yankees baseball cap, gun holstered and concealed under his windbreaker. The tip was good because a mousy guy in baggy clothes and a denim jacket loitered near the dumpster that filled an alley to the side of the deli.

"In position," Zach said into his radio.

"Ten-four," Noah replied. "I got eyes on him, too. We'll move in if Eddie alerts."

Zach and Eddie made their way to the shop window, peering in as if they were planning out a purchase. A whiff of yeast-scented steam tickled their noses. The shop was crammed with people grabbing up morning coffee and shouting out their orders for bagels to the unflappable guy behind the counter. Poppy seed, cinnamon raisin, hard salt, accompanied by dozens of different spreads from cream cheese and lox, to whitefish, to pimento-olive spread. Zach kept his peripheral vision on the alley.

He bent to scratch the dog. "Find the drugs, Eddie."

Eddie sprang into action, tail zinging as Zach walked him by the guy in the alley who was lighting a cigarette. Eddie sniffed in the direction of the man's boots, his body tensing in that way that promised a bust was going to go down. He pointed his nose at

Victor's pockets, precise as a laser beam locked on target.

The man looked up, startled, just as Eddie sat down at his feet. Zach pulled his gun. "Police. Let me see your hands."

In moments Noah was there, and Gavin, too, who had been positioned a few blocks from their location. Zach patted the man down and retrieved his wallet, identifying him as Victor Jones, along with an eight ball of cocaine, three and a half grams, wrapped neatly for easy distribution. It wouldn't fetch much, probably a hundred dollars or less, but it was plenty. While Gavin cuffed Jones, Zach gave Eddie a few of the coveted treats from his pouch. The dog munched happily, celebrating a job well-done.

"You're under arrest," Gavin said, before he Mirandized Jones.

Jones grunted. "C'mon, man. I can't do jail time now. I got bills to pay and my girl's gonna dump me if I serve time now."

"Your girl should dump you, anyway, if

she knows what's good for her," Zach said. "You sell drugs. She can do better." Zach waited a few beats as Victor wriggled in the handcuffs. "But I'm a softie so maybe there's something we can do, work out some kind of a deal."

Victor raised a wary eyebrow. "What kind of deal?"

"Information. You share it with me, and I can talk to the DA, maybe get you off easier."

Victor's body went tense. "Don't have any information."

"Aww, come on, Vic. Don't waste my time, man. We know you've been working with someone at LaGuardia who gets you and the drugs through security. Who is it?"

Terror sparked in Victor's eyes. He shook his head. "Dunno anything about that. I'm a homebody. I don't like airplanes."

"Not buying it, Victor. You flew on Emerge Airline three times the last month alone. You're smuggling for someone. I want the name."

"Like I said, I can't help you."

Zach stood a little closer. "Yes, you can. One name."

Victor's throat muscles worked but he remained mute.

Zach heaved an elaborate sigh. "I tried. You'll be going to jail now. You can say goodbye to your girl." He pretended to be thinking it over. "Hey, this is your second strike, so you're getting close to prison time, aren't you? Another drug charge isn't going to look good for you."

A bead of sweat slid down Victor's cheek. "Don't you have other people to hassle? I'm small-time."

Zach closed in like a shark smelling blood in the water. "But you can give me the big-time guy. Who are you smuggling for, Victor?" *Bill Oscar.* Zach was ready for Victor to spill the name. One word and he'd put Violet's boss away before he could threaten her safety any further. He stepped forward even farther, crowding Victor, and Eddie whined. Noah shot Zach a look. With an effort, Zach remained calm. "I've got things to do, Victor. We can't stand here forever. One name, that's all."

Victor chewed his lip. "Can't tell you, man."

"Why not?" Zach snapped. "If you don't, you'll go to jail for a long time."

"Better than crossing him."

"Who?" Zach demanded. "Give me the name and we'll protect you."

"Yeah, right." Victor guffawed. "'Cause the cops are so good at protecting people they want to toss in jail. Uh-uh. I don't work for anybody, and I ain't giving you nothing. Take me to jail now and let's stop wasting both our time."

Zach grunted and started to question Victor further when Noah gripped his bicep.

"Let it go for now. He may be more inclined to talk after he sits in a cell for a while."

Stomach tight with fury, Zach led Eddie away. Anger coursed through him in unrelenting waves, though he tried to calm himself. He knew Victor and Beck and Roach had to be working for or through Bill Oscar. It was the perfect setup. Bill ushered them through the airport, being sure they checked in during his shift. They bypassed security via the crooked TSA guy, Jeb Leak, who had so far avoided arrest, and Bill reaped the profits. Could be Bill was working with a big-time dealer, Uno or someone else, but he was the key, Zach was certain. All he needed was confirmation from Victor...and he hadn't gotten it. He would try again after Victor cooled his heels in a cell for a couple of hours.

The flood of people exiting the store with their bagels passed by, oblivious to him and Eddie. The sun was unusually warm for

May, and Eddie was basking against a brick wall, soaking in the beams after enjoying his treat. Dogs had an enviable ability to relax no matter what the circumstances. With Violet intending to return to work the next day, he felt anything but relaxed. Another chance to nail Bill Oscar had slipped right through his fingers.

Next best step. The words came to him unbidden, Jordy's favorite saying. When the wheels fell off the wagon and everything about a case was coming apart bolt by bolt, his big brother would say the only option was to take the "next best step." For the first time since Jordy's death, he was able to enjoy the memory without a stab of agony. There was pain, yes, probably always would be, but there was also a bit of gentle comfort in the replaying of his brother's wisdom. He had that to hold on to, if nothing else.

The sun was mellowing into a perfect

spring morning. He felt a ferocious yearning to run along the Vanderbilt Parkway and breathe in the sights and smells of the city like he'd done so many times with Jordy, but he knew that place would forever be ruined by the image of his dead brother, back against the tree. What had been his last thoughts as he'd died? Sadness that he was alone without a single soul to share his last moments? Zach swallowed down the anguish. There would be time for rest later, after he got Bill behind bars. Before that happened, he had another difficult mission to attend to: convincing Violet that she should take some vacation time, a leave, anything until he figured out the truth about Bill.

Violet was, above all things, loyal, so he'd have his hands full with that endeavor. Somehow he would find a way to reason with her. He looked at Eddie. "Got any good tips on how to handle a tough woman who isn't about to listen to good sense?"

Eddie opened one eye and then closed it again.

"Yeah, that's what I thought. Let's go, Eddie. Time to try and move a mountain."

NINE

Fatigue dulled Violet's senses, though it was only just past the breakfast rush. She had been awake since 3 a.m., long before her muffin drop at the Jamesons', thanks to the whining of a certain Labrador puppy. She'd finally strong-armed her parents into letting her go to the diner, promising to get a police escort when she returned to check on Latte. To her chagrin, a plainclothes detective had been assigned to be her babysitter, unless Zach or another member of the K-9 unit was available.

Even without the shrill puppy whining, she would have been awake, anyway. She hadn't slept past eight o'clock more than a handful of times in her entire life. The early bird got the extra puppy shifts and she'd spent the predawn hours in between doggie playtime sessions searching her mother's cookbooks for the perfect lemon meringue pie recipe.

Now, back at home for another round of midmorning puppy care, her thoughts traveled again to pie. It still irked Violet that she could not seem to master the art of making her mother's favorite pie, no matter how she went about it. Every time she attempted one, the meringue would shrink and pull away from the crust or the custard would be too loose or too firm. Her father had always said the best way to get Violet to attempt a task was to tell her she couldn't do it. He was right, and she was doggedly determined to make a perfect pie for her mother's birthday party on Tuesday. Killers and threats and fear were not going to derail her from her self-appointed mission.

Her mother's old cookbooks were yellowed and worn—obsolete, since there were millions of recipes online—but some things were better off old-school style. Violet put a sticky note on the page in the book that had belonged to her grandmother, with the handwritten, "Scrumptious!" note scrawled next to the ingredients. If it was scrumptious enough for Grandma, it would be good enough for Mom, and maybe she could even get Zach to eat some. She closed the book as she heard Latte clamoring for attention from his pen.

Latte seemed to operate at full speed as soon as his eyes popped open. Even after three different ball-chasing sessions and a full-body grooming, he was alert as ever. Lying on his back in his gated area of the kitchen, he was happily chewing on his rubber bone, having upended his water since she last checked. He righted himself and leaped at the gate when he spotted her, tail zinging as if he hadn't played with her in days instead of minutes.

"You're a wild one," she said, lifting the

roly-poly puppy over the gate. "I don't know how Ellie and Carter keep up with your two siblings." His pink tongue lapped her everywhere he could reach, and her problems melted away, if just for a moment. Was it humanly possible to sustain negative feelings while holding a warm puppy? She did not think so. Cuddling him and addressing him in outrageous baby talk that she'd never indulge in if others were present, she led the wriggling armful of joy outside to do his business again. Zach had admonished her in that annoying cop way of his that there was to be no taking the dog for walks in their quiet neighborhood unless he was present. Instead, she settled for playing a comical game of fetch with Latte, who would pounce on the ball eagerly, but could not be persuaded to return it to her. So far the count was five balls stored up in a pile across the yard and one left in the toy basket ready to throw.

"You're just not getting this fetch thing down, are you, Latte?"

"If only we could get the bad guys to carry around tennis balls," a voice said. "The dogs would catch them in no time."

She whirled around to find Zach leaning against the wall of the porch, arms folded, one booted ankle crossed over the other. Eddie wagged his tail and yipped at Latte. The sun lit Zach's eyes to a vivid cobalt. He was not in uniform, but his badge was clipped to his belt. Long, lean, but not entirely relaxed.

Her stomach fluttered, and she was glad she'd taken the time to shower that morning and pull her hair back into a neat ponytail. "I didn't hear you knock."

"That's 'cause I didn't. Your mother said I can let myself in the backyard anytime to let Eddie and Latte have a playdate if he isn't already booked with his puppy brothers and sisters."

"That's because she doesn't want you in the house. You break too many things."

"Nope, it's because your mother adores me, and you know it."

She did, too. Barbara Griffin loved the Jameson boys as if they were her own sons. In a way, they were, since they had spent their formative years with Violet's brother, Bobby. The hallway was lined with pictures of the six of them, Jordan, Noah, Zach, Carter, Bobby and Violet, in various stages of growing up, only Bobby's image had disappeared from the family photos too early. What would he have been like as an adult? she wondered. Would he be a cop, too? Married? A father? Again, the fuzziness of her memories of Bobby bothered her. It was as if he was fading from the pages of her mind like old photos exposed to sunlight.

Shake off those thoughts, she told herself firmly, wishing Zach did not look quite so appealing, sunlit and smiling. "You look… edgy," she said.

"Who, me? Nah."

She arched an eyebrow. "You can fool other people, but not me. You're edgy. Why?"

He shrugged, releasing Eddie to play with Latte. "We arrested Victor Jones, and I was hoping he'd roll over on his boss."

"But he didn't?"

"Not so far." Zach cleared his throat. "Threat's still out there."

She didn't answer.

"I know a guy," he said over the canine greetings. "He works at JFK and he…"

"No." There was no way she was going to transfer her job to another airport.

"But it would be…"

"Uh-uh, and we're not having this conversation again." She marched into the kitchen and poured a cup of coffee.

"Vi, why won't you see reason?"

"Because I'm not going to let anyone run

me out of my job. I like it and I'm good at it."

"Your boss is likely involved with drug dealers, or he's running an operation himself."

"I just can't make myself believe it. I know he must have reasons for doing what he did, good ones."

"That's because you're loyal and stubborn and it's given you a blind spot."

She dashed milk in the coffee, splashing some over the rim. "Fine, I'll own that, but I'm not judging Bill guilty until I have proof, and if I'm working at LaGuardia I can be your eyes and ears. We can clear the whole thing up for good."

"That is a terrible idea, so get that out of your head right now. Bill's dealing with bad people like Xavier Beck."

She repressed a shiver. "I learned a lesson last night. It was stupid of me to leave the apartment, but now I'm going to keep my eyes open and not take any chances. I'll be perfectly fine in a public airport."

"What if things go bad? Beck's tough."

She recalled her fear with Beck in the dank basement. She thrust her chin up, anyway. "I'm tough."

"He's tougher."

"You're wrong."

"I'm hardly ever wrong."

She shoved the mug of coffee at him. "You say that because you are loyal and stubborn and it's given you a blind spot about me."

He shook his head and, to her surprise, actually chuckled.

"Why the laugh when I just told you off?"

"You're the only person I know who would shoot me down thoroughly with my own words and make coffee for me at the same time."

She could not stop her own smile. "I don't do that for everyone, you know. Consider yourself a blessed man."

She'd aimed for flippant, but the look he

gave her was suddenly tender and thoughtful, exasperation and bemusement that resolved into a shining certainty. "I do," he said quietly. "I'm not sure how I can say that with the present circumstances of my life, but you're right. I'm blessed, where you're concerned, even though Jordy always said we fight like an old married couple."

Where you're concerned, as if she was something precious and rare that outshone the darkness cloaking him. The notion warmed her inside and eased warmth into her cheeks. *Lord, help me give him what he needs to push through the pain, to find his way back to You.*

"So what do you say, Vi? Will you consider the JFK thing? Please? For me?" It was not the little-boy-lost manner he sometimes employed to get her to agree. Sincerity teased tenderness into his tone. Oh, how tempting it was to give in, when she knew her assent would ease his strain. *Give in. Let him take care of you.* But then what would be next? Moving back in permanently with her parents? Starting over as a newbie when she'd worked hard for her seniority at LaGuardia? Worst of all, handing her independence to a man who did not love her in the way she craved? "I'm still not going to quit my job," she said. "Tomorrow I'll be back to work."

He exhaled deeply. "Yeah, I figured that's what you'd say." He drank from the mug and sighed. "You make good coffee, Vi, the best I've ever tasted."

"I know. It's in my blood. Griffins are born with coffee in their veins."

He grinned. "Cops, too."

"Otto used to say the same thing."

He looked down for a moment. "Ah, well, sorry I brought up bad memories."

"They aren't bad. Otto was a good guy, just not the one for me. The whole thing taught me that I need to take care of myself."

Zach looked at her full-on. "Violet, Otto was insane to let you go."

She offered a casual shrug, though the words thrilled her. *Keep your head, Vi. You didn't feel the right things for Otto. Like the things you feel for Zach?* Pouring herself a cup of coffee to give herself something to do, she clinked mugs with his.

Zach grinned. "You know what I found in an old box when we were packing up Jordy's stuff?"

"What?"

"A picture of that infamous Fourth of July."

She knew exactly the one. "Oh, boy. I'd forgotten about that."

"Not me. That was the best ambush in Jameson family history." His eyes twinkled with mischief. "And you were the perfect accomplice."

"I still feel guilty about it."

"No way. My brothers had it coming. They swiped the keys to my car and moved it so I thought it was stolen, remember? I ran around like an idiot for hours until they returned it just before the cops arrived, which made me look like an even bigger dummy. Oh, they had it coming and you were my wingman."

She sighed. "Yeah. I lured them all out into the backyard with the promise of chocolate chip cookies and you unleashed, what, like two dozen water balloons?"

"Oh, three dozen at least, and because I was standing on the roof at the time, they couldn't escape. It was perfect. I laughed so hard I almost slid off. That was a classic moment that I'll never forget."

"I don't know how I let you talk me into that."

"Aww—" he tugged at her sleeve "—it's because I'm irresistible and you can't say no to me, right?"

He had no idea how close he was to the truth.

Assorted barks and yips drew them to the back door, where they stood, sipping coffee and watching Eddie and Latte race merry circles around each other. It was a moment of peace to be enjoyed shoulder to shoulder. Precious seconds with a precious man. For just a fraction of a minute, she imagined what it would be like if Zach was hers, and she his…like the married couple Jordy suggested, sharing a space, sharing a life, their picture on the wall with all the others.

No good thinking that. Friends, remember?

When they finished, she took his coffee cup and rinsed it.

"I can do that," he said.

"I'm faster. I've got to secure Latte and scoot to the diner. Mom and Dad need me for the lunch rush. Nice weather will bring people out in droves."

"I'll drive you."

"Okay, I'll let you."

He twirled her ponytail, his fingers grazing the back of her neck, teasing prickles across her skin. "Always the tough lady."

Not always, she thought, as she considered that the next day she'd be walking back into the lion's den.

But his touch, warm and reassuring, pushed the danger and every other thought to the back of her mind.

Friends, remember?

Scooping up the pup, she escaped upstairs.

"Victor Jones made bail before I finished my lunch."

Noah's words grated in Zach's gut the next afternoon as he and Eddie drove the New York streets.

Victor had been bailed out by a relative without confirming or denying that he'd been working for Bill Oscar. Now Violet was at work, against all common sense and his strongest efforts at persuasion, and he was still not a bit closer to bringing down her boss. At least he'd managed to get Victor's last known address in Queens, an illegal basement apartment on a busy intersection in Corona. Armed with a search warrant, he forced the landlord to let him into the space, which was not zoned for residential use. He'd refer that one to the housing bureau later.

Zach eased his way into the basement and flipped on the light. A futon with rumpled sheets occupied the darkest corner. A card table served as a kitchen counter, cluttered with empty Chinese-take-out containers crusted with dried noodles, a hot plate and a coffee machine, a phone-charger cord, a strip overloaded with plugs. Such was the problem with illegal apartments. One exit in case of fire, and way too many safety violations. The space also lacked appropriate ventilation, but with affordable housing so hard to come by in Queens, the temptation to rent out unsafe rooms was hard to resist. Eddie whined.

The landlord stood by the door, arms crossed defiantly. Gavin had arrived to assist, and he kept a careful eye on the man.

So did Tommy, Gavin's springer spaniel, who was sitting obediently at his knee, tracking every movement.

"You have no right to come in here," the landlord snapped.

"The search warrant and the badge say otherwise," Zach said.

"My tenant has done nothing."

Zach rounded on him. "Your *tenant* is a drug dealer and if I find anything illegal in this basement you call an apartment, I'm going to find him and he'll go to prison. Would you like to join him there for interfering with an investigation? You already have enough problems, I'm thinking."

The landlord took a step forward, but Gavin raised a warning finger. "You're gonna stay out of this or I will cuff you right now, you got me?"

The landlord shot him a surly glare and retreated. Zach beamed Gavin a grateful look. "Now, where were we, Eddie?"

But Eddie was turning in agitated circles, his ears flapping.

"What do you smell?" He unclipped the dog. "Ready to work? Find the drugs, boy."

Eddie pranced into action, nosing along one wall, which was inexpertly covered with cheap wood paneling. Eddie paced back and forth along the paneling until he honed in on one particular spot. Zach's pulse thumped as Eddie's nose quivered, deciphering a thousand smells that Zach was not even aware of. Eddie finally sat and looked at him.

Gavin watched. "He got something?"

"I believe he does." Zach knelt next to him and examined the wood, rapping his knuckles every few inches. The sound echoed hollowly at the point where Eddie was most interested. Sliding on gloves, he edged a penknife in the notch between the sheets of paneling. Almost invisible to the eye, he found a tiny indentation where the wood had been filed away. Zach's gut tightened in anticipation. "Well, what do we have here?"

Using his knife as a lever, he popped the paneling loose. It came away easily. Eddie barked. Zach peered into the space where the drywall had been cut away. A stack of plastic-wrapped bricks—cocaine, no doubt—and a half dozen guns were jammed in the small alcove.

Gavin looked over his shoulder and whistled. "Dog's got a million-dollar nose, that's for sure."

"Yeah, he does. Good boy, Eddie. That's my baby," he said, doling out treats to the dog. "You did it again." The street value of the drugs was probably somewhere in the neighborhood of a half a million dollars.

Gavin radioed their findings and began taking photos. "So Victor is clearly moving product for someone," he said in between shots. "Why would he risk getting popped at the bagel store?"

Zach's thoughts spun as he turned the situation over in his mind. "He needs money. They've had to slow down their operation since Violet pointed out Beck at the airport. I think Victor was desperate for cash and kept a little to sell on the street for his own profit until he has the all-clear to start moving it again. His boss wouldn't like it, so he's kept his borrowing small."

"This supply is a lot to walk away from. Victor must intend to come back here at some point. He wouldn't abandon it, or his boss would make him pay."

Make him pay...

Just like he intended to do with Violet?

With Victor cut loose from jail and their stash discovered, would his boss order him to make another threat on Violet? Their need to keep the product moving must be growing.

He reached for his phone and left Gavin and another newly arrived officer to secure the scene and wait for the evidence to be processed. Scrambling back to his vehicle, he phoned Violet.

"Answer, answer," he said. He had to tell her that another one of the frequent fliers was involved in heavy-duty crime, probably organized by her boss. One ring, two. It went to voice mail.

He phoned Griffin's.

Barbara answered, sounding harried.

"I need to talk to Violet. Is she there?"

"No, Zach. Bill asked her to come in for an early shift today, so she left here hours ago for the airport."

His lungs struggled to do their job.

"She had a cop escort her, and she texted me that she'd arrived safely. Is there a problem?"

He forced a cheerful tone. "No, ma'am. I just…need to talk to her."

Her voice dropped low. "Zach, we're counting on you to take care of our daughter."

"Yes, ma'am. I will do that. I promise."

Barbara said goodbye and hung up, though she did not sound completely convinced.

He gunned the engine on the Tahoe and pushed out into traffic, goosing the gas and flipping on the siren.

Bill couldn't make a move to hurt Violet in the airport in front of dozens of witnesses. She was probably safe…as long as Zach could get there in time.

TEN

Violet was happy to steep herself in the madness of her ticket counter duties again. Puppy care was fun but exhausting and though her father complained about her decision, she'd kissed him and left him muttering over his vat of vegetable beef soup. As usual, her mother did not give voice to her worry, but it was evident in the tensing of her shoulders.

I've got to live my life, she wanted to say, *to take care of myself.* Killers and her burgeoning feelings for Zach aside, she really was okay on her own, and that was the way she would keep it, no matter who tried to strip it away from her.

Bill had greeted her upon her arrival with

a quick hug. "Happy to see you back here, young lady. You look rested and raring to go."

"Put me in, Coach," she'd said with a smile before she was sucked into the busy whirl of airport duty.

There was nothing unusual transpiring that Violet could detect, just the typical crush of people, some anticipating a vacation trip or reunion, and those more surly, traveling on business or for some other less enjoyable reason. Bill's wife, Rory, phoned in the afternoon and asked to speak to Violet during her break.

"I am so sorry about what happened," she said. "It's horrible. Bill has been so worried about you. He's hardly sleeping, and I think he's started smoking again. He tries to hide it, but I can smell it on his clothes."

"I'll tell him to stop if I catch him with cigarettes in his pocket. We'll get him back on track." Violet pictured Rory the last time she'd seen her, the shadows that smudged

Rory's eyes and her thinning hair, which had once been a thick chestnut brown. "How are you doing with the treatments? I know it's been tough."

Rory's sigh spoke of exhaustion. "Seems like the cure is worse than the disease sometimes. The doctor is optimistic. It's hard on the boys, though. I'm the one that keeps things on an even keel, normally, because Bill works such long hours. They don't quite understand how to deal with me being sick." She coughed and cleared her throat. "He doesn't, either. He tries, but it's hard for him to know what to say, how to be, so most of the time he pretends nothing is going on. And the bills, they worry him, too. He doesn't sleep hardly at all and he's lost weight."

"Have you… I mean, he's been a bit different at work. Something is definitely on his mind. Could there be something besides the treatments weighing on him?"

Rory paused a moment. "No, he's just

stressed is all, and who wouldn't be?" She offered directions on some schoolwork to one of her children. "Anyway, I wanted to thank you for the flowers you sent last week and to be sure you're okay."

"Perfectly okay, thanks."

"Good. You're like family, Violet, and we'd be crushed if anything happened to you." Rory bade her goodbye. As Violet disconnected, she eyed Bill smiling at a customer. Surely Bill would not entangle himself with the drug trade. He would never do that to his wife and sons.

Bill walked around the counter and joined her after the next shift of workers arrived. He looked fatigued, twitchy. Of course he'd been off his game a little, she thought. His whole life was his family and with a thing like cancer to deal with… Guilt swelled inside her for her earlier suspicion.

I misjudged him. He couldn't have been helping Beck.

"Rory was sweet to call," she said. "She's such a thoughtful person."

"Rory's one in a million. When I married her, I won the grand prize. She's way better than I deserve."

She caught just a whiff of tobacco on his clothes. "You've been smoking again, haven't you?"

Head ducked, he sighed. "I had one or two this morning before I got here, but I'll stop, I promise. A moment of weakness."

"Why, Bill? What is worrying you, and don't say it's all Rory because you're not that good at lying."

"I'm better than you think," he said morosely.

"What does that mean?"

He shoved his hands in his pockets. "Vi, will you come have coffee with me?"

"Sure, that'd be great sometime."

"I mean now."

"Why now?"

"Your shift is done, and I'm taking the

rest of the day off. I know this nice coffee shop in Astoria, a café, really, and I don't want to waste this sunny afternoon. Who knows when we'll get another one. Let me treat you before you head home."

"Some other time, maybe?"

"Please," he said, gaze drifting across the terminal. "I... There's some things I need to get off my chest."

She felt a prickle of alarm. "Why can't we talk here? We can grab some coffee in the lounge. It's terrible, I know, but it's usually hot."

He did not return her smile. "I need to speak privately with you. An hour, that's all. I promise it won't take longer than that."

Still, she hesitated.

"Vi, I've known you a long time. You know my wife, my boys. You've come to their baptisms, their school plays. You've been at our place for barbecues and my wife's jewelry-selling parties or whatever it is she arranges. You're family and it kills me to think you don't trust me anymore."

Anguish pinched the corners of his mouth. It was genuine emotion, she was sure of it. He was in desperate trouble, she could sense it. "I know you're a good man and a good father, Bill."

His smile was wan. "Well that's something, anyway. Does that warrant an hour of your time? Sixty minutes, tops? We'll stay in a public place and come right back."

She knew without a doubt that Zach would not want her going anywhere with Bill, but his expression was so downcast, she could not believe he might be the mastermind of a drug-smuggling operation. Besides, Astoria in late afternoon would be bustling, especially on such a warm day, and she did not think it would put her in any danger to have coffee with Bill. If her instincts were right, he would tell her something she could share with Zach to help him put Beck behind bars. It might be the only chance to put an end to the chaos.

"All right," she said. "Let me get my purse."

His face lit with a relieved grin. "Excellent. I'll get us a car."

Violet snatched her purse from behind the counter and sent Zach a text, noting she had a missed call from him.

Going to coffee with Bill in Astoria. Have to hear him out.

She waited, the seconds ticking by, hoping he would reply.

Bill was standing, checking his watch. Still no answer from Zach.

She made a pretense of fixing her lipstick.

"Ready?" Bill called.

Her phone screen remained blank. Doubt assailed her. She could still make an excuse, change her mind.

"Gotta get going," Bill said.

"All right." She slipped the phone into her pocket and followed him out of the terminal.

Twenty minutes later they sat on a curbside bench with their coffees since all the tables were occupied. The bench edged a wall, near the corner of two busy streets, so they sipped as a parade of pedestrians strolled by, the city bustling in all its glory.

Violet was comforted by the busyness. She relaxed just a bit in the sunshine and sipped the strong brew. It was hot and slightly bitter, not as good as Griffin's coffee, she thought Zach would say.

Bill shifted on the bench, toying with his cup but not drinking.

"What did you want to tell me, Bill?"

He grinned. "That's what I like about you, Vi. You're a 'get to the point' gal. No small talk."

"My feet are aching to be put up at home." She tried for a teasing tone but his smile had vanished, leaving his expression grim.

Stomach knotted, she rested the coffee cup on her knee, tension boiling up in her stomach.

"Vi, I want to apologize in advance for what I've got to tell you."

She straightened and took a bracing breath. Whatever Bill Oscar had to confess, it wasn't going to be good.

Zach had screeched to the curb at the airport just in time to see Violet and Bill pull away in a cab. Her earlier text, the one he'd only recently read, was alarmingly short.

She had not replied to his answering string of messages that ended with "Do NOT go anywhere with him. Wait for me." Of course she hadn't waited. Violet "I can handle myself" Griffin. If it wasn't so maddening, it would make him smile, this woman who would go toe-to-toe with anyone. In their high school days, he'd actually seen her use a broom to chase away a teen who'd been intent on graffitiing the wall of the diner. She'd probably make an excellent defender if she ever had the yen to join his police basketball team. He'd jokingly asked her before, and she'd replied with a sassy, "Not in this lifetime. Your uniforms are way too ugly."

He tried to tail them, a maddening prospect in city traffic, staying far enough back in his squad car that he hoped Bill hadn't noticed. With each congested mile his pulse ticked higher. He mentally practiced the points he would make when he chewed her out. It would be helpful to prep ahead of time, since she could talk circles around him when she had a mind to, but there could be no justifying getting into a cab with Bill Oscar.

He'd lost them a few times, but finally trailed them to a coffee shop. The block was dotted with eateries, everything from Greek dolmas, Hawaiian poke, cheese blintzes, and Vietnamese noodles in rich broth. Eddie's nose twitched as he sampled the air.

"I know, I'm hungry, too. Work first, lunch later." Though he was certain Eddie questioned his priorities, he flapped his ears and continued their slow amble around the coffee shop, searching for a place to park, which had added a maddening amount of time.

He'd taken a moment to pull a plain jacket over his uniform shirt, take off his utility belt in favor of a sidearm holster and tug on a Yankees baseball cap. He put a civilian harness on Eddie and slid on a pair of sunglasses before they made their way briskly back to the café.

After completing their second casual stroll around the shop, and finding nothing amiss, he pretended to study the menu written on a chalkboard easel, keeping Bill and Violet in his sight every moment.

Bill's shoulders were tensed, knee bobbing as he sat on the bench, close to Violet but not touching her, squinting against the sun. For her part, Violet seemed attentive, but not alarmed as far as he could tell, one elegant leg crossed over the other, peep-toed high heels adding a trademark sense of style to her navy blue airline skirt and jacket.

Bill seemed to be talking in stops and starts, nervous, clearly. Was he trying to convince her of his innocence, or confessing his guilt? Irritation and fear raked through him again. The guy could very well be a drug dealer and Violet was coolly sipping coffee with him like he was a long-lost uncle. He could have called his people to arrange a hit, or an abduction, and Violet would have no place to hide. The thought made Zach's muscles bunch into knots.

Calm down, he told himself. A tall order, even on a good day.

Zach had never been sedate. During their tutoring sessions, when Jordy helped Zach study for the police exam, they'd taken breaks every half hour, shooting hoops, doing pushups, playing with the dogs, anything to stem Zach's restlessness and frustration that came with long hours of wrestling with his dyslexia. Books made him fidgety. He'd much rather listen to them on audio while running a couple of miles.

Reining you in is like trying to saddle a wild horse, Jordy had lamented many times. Since Jordy's murder, Zach's emotions seemed to be uncontainable, breaking loose in spite of his efforts to subdue them. Embarrassing, humiliating, but the emotions would not go away no matter how hard he squashed them down.

Why had God taken away his brother?

It's okay that you're struggling with Jordy's death...it's healthy to talk about it.

No, it wasn't. Violet was wrong. Unbridling all that mess made him less of a cop, less of a man. Bill fidgeted. Zach was once again furious at the guy who'd landed Violet knee-deep in threats.

Rage threatened to gallop away with him. He had to force himself not to charge that bench and march Violet right on her sleek high heels back to his squad car. Instead, he pulled the baseball cap down and meandered closer, slouching against a nearby lamppost as if he was texting someone. Cell phones tended to trap people in bubbles of oblivion, but they could be a cop's best friend…or a killer's.

At that moment Violet looked up, riveting her brown gaze to his. She startled just a little, but to her credit, she covered it by tucking her hair back into the clip that held the mass of curls at the nape of her neck. His look no doubt telegraphed, *What exactly do you think you are doing?* but she moved her attention back to Bill. She could feel his ire, no doubt, and he figured she was going to have to bake him a whole batch of apple pies to make up for this silly stunt. He strained to hear their conversation.

"…got you into this mess," Bill was saying. The words sounded earnest enough, the body language seemed to match, but

Zach didn't believe it, not one single syllable. He hoped Violet didn't, either. He scanned the crowd again. Had Bill alerted Beck? Was he snaking his way along the sunny sidewalk toward Violet? But no one seemed at all interested in the two chatting on the bench. A lady edged by him, clutching a cell phone to one ear and toting a paper-lined basket with a club sandwich and chips. Eddie tracked the tantalizing scent. She found a seat under one of the orange umbrellas. A man in a business suit joined her, pressing a kiss to her cheek before he sat. Just people out enjoying the spring sunshine, not threats. Zach bent over to scratch Eddie, which gave him an excuse to shuffle a few inches closer.

"Debts," Bill was saying.

The word caught Zach's attention.

"Rory's care is so expensive, and our medical benefits aren't what they used to be. And the kids, I mean, their private school costs a mint, but I can't uproot them now, can I? Not with their mother being so sick. All their friends are there, and Rory would be heartbroken if we pulled them out. I'd get another job, but after forty years with an airline, I don't know how to do anything else. I've worked at the airport since I was sixteen."

Violet caught his wrist. "What are you saying, Bill? Quit dancing around it."

Zach could see the coffee cup trembling in his fingers. "I… I thought it would be a quick way to earn some money to pay for Rory's treatments and the kids' expenses. I promise you I never wanted anyone to get hurt."

Violet's voice was calm and measured. "Tell me the truth, all of it."

"I can't. It's too dangerous."

"We're way past that," Violet snapped. "I almost got killed. My house is under police watch and I can't even sit on the front stoop."

Atta girl, Vi, Zach thought with a smile. *Stay strong. Don't fall for his sympathy act.*

Bill rubbed a palm on his jeans. “I’m so sorry, but there’s no way I can fix it. You should leave things alone, Vi. Just forget the whole thing and get your cop friend to back off. Leave town, maybe. Just for a while until this all blows over.”

“I’m not going anywhere, Bill, so you might as well just spit it out. What happened at the airport? What are you a part of?”

He toyed with the lid of his cup. “The guy you fingered, Xavier Beck, he’s bad news. Ruthless, cunning.”

No newsflash there, Zach thought.

“People who threaten him don’t survive. He wants to impress his boss, and he’ll go after you to clean up the mess at the airport because you’re a threat. You’re a witness to him smuggling drugs. You’ve seen his face.”

What boss? Zach risked edging a few inches closer. This might be a story Bill had cooked up to protect his own skin. Or perhaps the hints about a bigger boss, Uno, were founded after all.

Violet skewered Bill with a look. “You’ve been allowing drugs to pass through the airport. Yes or no?”

Bill shoved his hands under his thighs. “Yes.”

Violet let out a breath and sagged a little. She’d wanted so badly to believe her boss and friend was not guilty.

“Oh, Bill,” she said. “I can’t believe you did that.”

“Me neither. Looking in the mirror now I don’t even recognize myself. It was small at first. Nothing major, a few ounces to test the system. I… I worked with Jeb Leak, the TSA guy, and we let Jones through, then Roach and Beck. As soon as I did it, I felt terrible, I wanted to stop, but Beck said he’d hurt my wife, my kids.” Bill’s voice caught. “What choice did I have, then? You’ve seen them, they’re vicious.”

A nice way to gain sympathy, bringing

in the wife and kids, Zach thought, but the fear rang true.

Violet stared at him. "Is this the truth, Bill, or are you lying to me? Who are you working for, exactly? Who is Beck's boss?"

He shook his head, scanning the street. "I've got no idea. They never told me and to be honest, I didn't want to know. I just wanted to get away from the whole nightmare and forget it ever happened."

"You must have an idea," she pressed.

"No, I..." Bill suddenly got to his feet.

Zach tensed and put his hand on the gun hidden under his jacket.

Bill dumped his coffee in the trash. "I've said too much. I don't want you to get hurt. Please do as I say. Don't ask any more questions. Find another job. I'll write you a recommendation, whatever you need. I'm sorry I got you involved. I never wanted things to be like this."

Bill extended a hand to Violet, clasping

her fingers in his. "I am truly sorry. I'll take you back now. This was a mistake."

A movement from across the street drew Bill's attention. He froze in place, hands still clasping hers, mouth open.

Zach moved forward to get a clearer view.

"No!" Bill yelled, leaping in front of Violet as gunfire erupted from across the street. Before Zach's gun cleared the holster, Bill was falling to the cement, a bullet hole punched in his right temple. He hit the sidewalk with a lifeless thud. A second and third bullet fractured the glass of the café, raining a torrent of gleaming shards.

Ambush, Zach's mind screamed as he dove for Violet.

ELEVEN

Zach had only a moment to squeeze off a shot at the assailant, a man wearing a black cap pulled down, short, barrel-chested—Xavier Beck, it had to be. Beck reeled back as Zach's shot skimmed his shoulder. Spinning, he took cover behind some parked cars.

Zach pulled Violet and Eddie inside the café. People were screaming, crying, so he had to yell to be heard. "NYPD. Everybody stay in here, and move away from the windows," he commanded. Then he radioed the dispatcher with the location, eyeing the parked cars across the street to see if he could take another shot. "Active shooter,

I need backup and an ambulance." Help would be rolling in seconds.

Violet did not appear to be injured, but she was breathing hard, face pale as milk.

"Tell me what to do," she whispered.

He gently pushed her toward the tables, farther away from the fractured windows. "Take Eddie. Keep him away from the glass and see if anyone is hurt."

As he'd suspected, giving her a task seemed to break through the shock. She nodded, accepted Eddie's leash without a word and crept from patron to patron.

He ran out into the street, crouched behind a newspaper stand, looking for the assailant. There was no sign of movement from across the street, but sirens wailed as the cavalry closed in. Would Beck flee? Or come at them in an effort to silence Violet? He'd be smart to run, but he'd already proved that there was no risk he would not take to get what he wanted. With no sign of Beck, he returned to the ruined café.

Go ahead, Beck. Make your move. I'm ready for you.

When the first officers arrived to tend to the victims, he filled them in as best he could. Violet continued her ministrations, making the rounds of the huddled diners, checking for injuries and reassuring them. The sirens were deafening now, wailing up the street, and in moments the area was awash in more cops and squad cars. It took several more moments for officers to organize and swarm the street, behind the parked cars and then into the nearby shops, clearing the spaces one by one. He joined them in the effort. With each shop they searched, his nerves hitched tighter. Where would Beck have gone? Where had he parked his motorcycle? Or had he come on foot, easily melting away into the crowd to make his escape? He could only relay his information to the arriving patrol officers and help in whatever way he could.

It was a good forty minutes before Noah

arrived, followed by Brianne Hayes and Luke Hathaway.

Noah had Zach and the other canine officers regrouped in the café for a debriefing, Scotty at his side, keeping the dog away from the broken glass.

"Nothing so far," Brianne Hayes said.

Noah looked at her. "I want you in on the interviews of the victims."

"Yes, sir." Her dog in training, Stella, the Lab, could encounter similarly traumatized people in her work as a bomb-detection dog. It would aid the dog in the future to gain experience from the shooting.

"We'll continue to canvass the area and assist the lieutenant in charge of the scene," Noah said. "He's asked us to move these witnesses to the building next door, away from all this glass while Brianne gets their statements."

Brianne nodded. "I'll handle it."

"I'll help," Luke put in.

"Where's your dog?" Brianne inquired.

"I came here directly from a class. Bruno's still in the kennel."

"I want to get Violet and Eddie away from here," Zach said. "Something doesn't feel right."

"Soon as we finish the secondary sweep, put Eddie in Luke's car. Violet can go in the front seat." Noah frowned at him, speaking lower so the others wouldn't hear. "Could have had mass casualties here, Zach. You should have arranged for backup before you tailed them to the café."

"I didn't know she was meeting Bill until just before this all went down. All I could think about was tailing Bill's car. Things went bad really fast."

"One radio call was all it would have taken to loop us in." He fingered his radio, a hard edge creeping into his tone. "That's why we have these things, you know. And safety protocols. I believe you've been trained in all that, correct? Perhaps a refresher course is needed?"

"Noah..." He fought down the adrenaline that made him want to bark at his brother. Not just his brother, his chief. He'd been brash, and he owed Noah an apology and the respect he deserved. "You're right, Chief. Sorry."

Noah quieted Scotty, who'd begun to whine. "Apology accepted, but I expect better next time. Let's do our jobs. You kept her and everybody else safe, so that's something."

But he hadn't kept Bill safe. He couldn't allow himself to mull over that at the moment. There would be plenty of time for analyzing his miscalculations later.

Violet was still walking around with Eddie in tow, talking in particular to an elderly lady until the medics took over to assess. Brianne and Luke began to herd the group from the café toward the side door that led to the next building. Noah was right. This could have been a scene of mass casualties, and Violet might have been one of them. He took her gently by the wrist and led her to a wooden chair, far away from the windows. "Wait for me here," he said to her. "Keep an eye on Eddie, okay?"

She nodded, and her meek compliance worried him.

He helped Noah and Brianne talk to witnesses that had been moved into the printing business. The manager had welcomed the victims warmly, offering bottles of water and folding chairs to the shocked patrons. New Yorkers might have the reputation for being tough-minded, but they took care of their own.

When everyone was settled as comfortably as they could be, he returned to the café, where a few officers were taping off the glass-strewn area and taking pictures. Violet sat on a chair, bent over, her cheek pressed to the top of Eddie's head. The sight of her cuddling his dog stopped him. She looked so small, so frightened, with her escaped curls draped along Eddie's face. It was as if she'd taken off the tough-girl cape, and now the soft, vulnerable woman underneath was visible. He was not sure how to take it, this new vision of a lifelong friend, but strange feelings overtook him.

"Hey," he said softly.

She bolted to her feet, twisting the leash between her fingers.

"It's okay. I didn't mean to startle you."

"I, uh…" She swallowed. "I mean, I think they just put Bill onto a stretcher. But…" Her lower lip trembled. "He's dead, isn't he, Zach?"

The sadness and uncertainty in her face cut at him. How he wanted to comfort her, to tell her some sort of fib that would take the pain away, but he would not ever lie to Violet Griffin. Not her, not ever.

"Yes, honey. He's dead. I'm sorry."

Her face crumpled and she began to cry, quiet sobs, fists clenched to her middle as if she was trying to hold the tears inside. His heart broke one inch at a time.

Eddie whined and pawed at her shoes.

Zach took her in his arms and held her, stroking her back and pressing a kiss to her temple, rocking her gently back and forth. "Aww, Vi. It's gonna be okay." How could he even say it when he'd doubted for the past month that the world would ever look right again? God was surely against him, cruel and comfortless, but with her there, pressed against his chest, he felt something different, which made him recall the words his mother had written in his Bible.

I will both lay me down in peace, and sleep: for thou, Lord, only makest me dwell in safety. Maybe his brain didn't believe it anymore, but he made his heart recite the words because, though Zach might not deserve peace or safety, Violet surely did.

God...help me believe it again. It was all he could say, the only thing he could pray.

Someone handed him a packet of tissues and he gave one to her. She pressed it to her face and choked out a few more gulping sounds. After a few moments he felt her straighten, and she faced him, swiping the tissue under her eyes.

"I know what you're thinking. I shouldn't have come here with Bill. You were right." New tears traced glistening trails on her cheeks. "Maybe if I hadn't..." Her mouth quivered again.

He cradled her cheeks between his palms and spoke quietly. "Violet, do not go there. Bill is not dead because of you. Beck shot him. Bill didn't want to cooperate anymore, and he'd become a liability to their operation so Beck murdered him and intended to take you out, too, if Bill hadn't shielded you. That's it."

"His wife, his boys." She bit her lip and he could see her fighting for control. She would not want to lose it here, not with the cops circling around.

He dried her tears with his thumbs. "We're leaving. I'll borrow Luke's vehicle to take us to my car. It's a couple of blocks from here. Brianne can help him retrieve his when they're done with the interviews."

She didn't respond, so he picked Eddie up and tucked him under one arm to carry him past the glass. His other hand he offered to Violet. She took it. "Your hands are freezing."

She mumbled something he didn't catch. Though she'd refused any medical attention, he resolved to keep a close eye on her for signs of shock. What she'd just witnessed would probably trouble her for many years to come. They exited the café and he purposefully stayed on her right side, to block her view of the bloodstained sidewalk. She clutched his fingers in a death grip as they went by.

"Keep walking, Vi. Look straight ahead."

When Eddie was secured in Luke's backseat, he urged her toward the front passenger door. "Sit in here for just a minute while I get a blanket out of the back."

He'd just grabbed the door handle to open

it for her, when a motorcycle roared up the street, ripping through the yellow caution tape.

The rider, Xavier Beck, had stripped off the cap, eyes burning like coals as he punched the motorcycle forward. Steering with one hand, he held a gun in his blood-stained other one. He bore down on them, firing wildly.

Zach had only a moment to throw himself on top of Violet and force her to the street.

The shots deafened her. Senses on overload, she could not process what was happening. Her arms and legs felt numb, her brain fuzzy. Someone, Zach, she realized, had pushed her down to the ground, shielding her with his torso as bullets peppered the asphalt around them. Sharp bits cut into her chin and the breath was squeezed out of her. Had she been shot? Had he? She could not be sure.

Then Zach pulled her to her feet, yanking her around the other side of the car, tugging her back inside the café, shouting into his radio. *We're still alive*, she told herself in disbelief. *Thank You, God.* Dimly, she heard Zach talking urgently into his radio.

"I've gotta get her out of here. I'll contact you when I can."

They sprinted out the back entrance and into an alley fetid with the smell of garbage and exhaust while cops surged all over the scene of the second shooting. She stumbled, but he helped her along. "We have to hurry, Violet. Beck made it past our guys. He's going to start tracking us if he can."

Terror made her blood run cold. Beck was coming. He'd killed Bill Oscar, her longtime friend, murdered him right on a public bench not three feet away. Now he was coming for her just like he'd promised in the airport. He wouldn't let her escape again. Icy prickles erupted along her spine. Suddenly, she could not pull any air into her lungs. She staggered to a stop, struggling against a growing dizziness.

He stopped, taking her by the arms, bending so he could look in her face. “We have to keep going.”

But she couldn’t. As much as she wanted to be strong, she simply could not force herself to move past the fear. It was as if her muscles and joints were paralyzed by a strange sort of inertia born of terror and helplessness.

Zach stroked her upper arms as if to warm her. “Vi, listen to me. I’m going to get you out of this. I’m going to keep you safe.” He smiled. “Just like when we were kids and you got stuck in that elm I told you not to climb in the Baisley Pond Park. You wouldn’t let anyone else help you down but me. Noah and Carter tried, and you screamed nonstop until I climbed up and got you. Remember that?”

She remembered. Staring into his eyes, blue as robins’ eggs, she recalled that moment when he'd commanded her to release the branch and hold on to him. *Let go, Violet. I won't let you fall.*

Now she tried to catch her breath and calm her terror. He would take care of her if she let him. She knew it with every cell in her being, just like she had as a child, perched on a limb, waiting for Zach and no one else. It felt to her then as though she'd been waiting for him her whole life, waiting to step out on that fragile branch that spanned the distance between the two of them.

"You trust me, don't you, Vi?"

She could not speak so instead she nodded. No matter what happened, how scared she felt, she would always trust Zach Jameson with everything.

"That's my Vi," he said, kissing her on the forehead. He reached behind her and untied her hair, freeing it from the scarf. For one breathless second, he trailed his fingers through her curls. "So you look a little different, harder to spot," he told her with a quirked smile. "Still gorgeous, just different."

Gorgeous? She felt anything but. The cut on her shin burned and sweat dampened her brow. Grit stuck to the palms of her hands and one of her shoe heels felt wobbly. She wiped off her hands and fixed her jacket.

Zach turned his baseball cap around backward. "We'll act casual. Head for a cab or the subway, something. You ready?"

"No, but I'll go with you, anyway."

He flashed one more grin. "Eddie will be sorry to be missing out on this adventure."

Her heart pounded as she suddenly remembered that Eddie was in the back of Luke's car. "Is he okay?" she asked as they hurried down the alley toward the sidewalk.

"Yeah, I heard him barking when we ran for the café. Luke will take care of him."

Police cars continued to pour into the area, sirens blasting. As they stepped from the alley onto the sidewalk, Violet's skin crawled. Was Beck still on his motorcycle, cruising the streets? Or was he on foot now, blending in with the pedestrians who rushed in every direction, panicked by the horrible act of violence that had occurred right around the corner?

Bill's last moments kept replaying in her mind, twisting her insides with pain. He'd been trying to fix his mistake, trying to warn her as best he could, just a man who'd fallen in with the wrong people, desperate to help his family. He'd risked his own safety to warn her, and it had cost him everything.

Zach pushed her through the agitated crowds until they were several blocks away. He radioed their location before he tucked her arm in his elbow and guided them quickly along. Her heart hammered so hard she was sure the frantic passersby could hear it. A scared woman elbowed past her and she nearly screamed, but Zach pressed her closer and sped up their pace. His expression was determined, calm. He appeared casual as he scanned the road traffic and the approaching people, but she knew he was taking in every detail. His fingers tightened around her wrist.

"There, across the street, nine o'clock."

She peeked past his shoulder and panic flooded her senses. Beck was standing across the street outside a corner grocery. He held one arm cradled to his body as he slowly perused the street.

Zach relayed Beck's location to the cops before he spoke to Violet. "He must have figured we'd ducked out the back. Keep moving. Don't speed up. We're one of the crowd," he whispered.

But Beck's perusal stopped as he fixed on them.

"He's spotted us, Zach," she said.

The aboveground subway station loomed over them. The flight of green stairs was dotted with stragglers hurrying to catch the next train. There was no time to wait for backup. Zach hesitated only a moment.

"We'll beat him to the subway."

"He'll catch us before we get there." Terror nearly blinded her.

"No, he won't." Zach grabbed her hand and they began to run.

TWELVE

He sprinted, Violet right next to him, amazingly agile even on high heels. Dodging past the crowds and earning some dirty looks, they reached the turnstiles.

"Zach," she panted, clutching at him. "I don't have my purse. I left it on the bench."

No purse meant no MetroCard. Zach wasted no time beelining to a transit official and flashing his badge. "We need to get through right now."

The heavyset officer asked no questions, just ushered them past the turnstile. They joined the people on the platform behind the yellow line, just as the train roared into the station. Zach tried to spot Beck. Had he had enough time to chase them down?

It seemed like the station was full of dark-clad men. He elbowed his way deeper into the crowd, putting his lips to her ear.

"If we get separated, make your way to this address." He mumbled it twice until she caught his collar and drew him closer.

"You're not leaving me."

"You'll get on the train and get away from here. I'll catch up with you later."

"Not going without you."

"If I spot him, I have to go after him, Vi. It's the only way to end this."

Her eyes burned and her lips tightened into a thin line. "Zach William Jameson, if you don't get onto this train with me I'll scream louder than I did from the top of that elm tree."

He wanted to laugh at her ferocious tone, but he knew it came from a place of deep fear. Would she be safer if he stayed behind and watched for Beck? But if the guy somehow managed to slip past him on the train, Violet would be completely unprotected.

He was reaching for his radio to update Noah when the people began to edge forward as the train doors slid open. Together or separate? She answered for him by grabbing his wrist and jerking him along until they were both bundled into the car. During the maneuver her high heel broke, but she hobbled along without missing a beat.

The jostling throng set his nerves firing as people crammed into the subway car. He'd never met a cop who felt comfortable in a closed space no matter what the circumstances, and he was no different. He swallowed against a wave of claustrophobia as the doors slid shut. Violet was unfazed, edging in and around the various passengers until she found an unoccupied seat on the end. She collapsed into it. Zach stood next to her, leaning on the silver pole, where he had a good view of every door, including the one to the adjoining car.

When the subway lurched out of the station, he shifted his focus completely to that spot. If Beck was on the train, he'd be coming through that entry point.

His anger hardened like forged steel. *Let him try.*

But with a subway car full of potential victims, he could not take any chances. He took out his phone and sent a text to Noah. He was beyond relieved to hear back that no one had been injured in Beck's secondary attack and Eddie would be safely delivered to the Jamesons' and an officer would retrieve Violet's purse. His second text was in the form of a request that went to his friend, Archie Ballentine, and the positive reply came back immediately. He heaved out a sigh.

"Where are we going?" Violet whispered.

He bent to keep their conversation private. "I know a guy in Manhattan, at the address I gave you earlier. We'll go to his place. It's safe there. He just confirmed."

She didn't speak; her demeanor was outwardly composed, but he knew it was a front. The tiny tremor in her fingers betrayed her. All he could do was stay glued to her side and keep his hand free in case he needed to reach for his gun.

After the twenty-minute ride, they switched trains, watching warily for signs that Beck was following. Violet and Zach saw one person came through the adjoining cars, an older woman with a tiny white dog nestled in her purse. She sat next to Violet in a seat that had been vacated along the way.

Violet offered her a wan smile.

The woman watched them for a long while before she finally quirked a brow at Violet and then at Zach. “Not my business, young man,” she said, “but you should take better care of your sweetheart. Her shoe is broken.”

Violet’s cheeks went red. “Oh, he’s not…”

“You’re right, ma’am,” Zach cut in. “It’s been an unusual day and I’ve been rushing her.”

"Unusual or not," she clucked, smoothing her wrinkled hands over her dog's wiry head. "You should never rush your sweetheart. And you've spent this whole ride staring at the door or your cell phone, not even giving one speck of attention to this beautiful lady."

"She's right," the woman across the aisle piped up. Zach swiveled to acknowledge her. She was bundled in a coat and rubber boots, sporting a chic red hat.

Violet's tiny smile indicated she was enjoying his public chastisement.

The look both women shot him was pure disapproval.

"Got to step up your game," the hat lady said, "if you want to keep her."

Zach felt like an insect on a pin as he cleared his throat. "Yes, ma'am."

"Women need to be treasured, pampered, treated like jewels." The older woman eyed Violet's broken shoe. "Well, you should take her someplace where she can have that shoe repaired and then get a bite to eat. I am quite certain I heard her stomach growl. It's nearly four o'clock. Did you even bother to get her lunch? A late-afternoon snack? Anything?"

"Uh, no, ma'am. We were..."

"I haven't eaten since breakfast," Violet said, her tone melancholy.

"What has happened to the youth in our country?" Huffing out a breath, the woman reached around the dog in her bag and pulled out a chocolate bar. "Eat this, honey. You need a pick-me-up, if this fellow did not so much as get you a hot dog for lunch."

With a sweet smile, Violet accepted. "Thank you very much. It's so kind of you."

The old woman shot Zach a hostile glare. "And don't share it with him until he learns some manners."

Zach was stumbling over some sort of reply when his phone buzzed with a text from Noah.

Beck's evaded capture. Watch your back.

He blew out a breath. At least Beck wasn't on the subway train. Now, if he could just get Violet to the safe house.

He looked up to find both women watching him, frowning.

"He can't even keep his eyes off his cell phone long enough for one conversation." Hat lady sniffed. "Pathetic."

"She could definitely do better," the older one said, launching into a story about her grandfather and his courtship procedures. He was beyond relieved when the train pulled into the station. Quickly, he took Violet's hand and helped her to her feet. She staggered a bit on her broken heel.

As Violet thanked the lady again for the candy bar, the woman handed her a slip of paper, whispering loud enough for him to hear, "My grandson is an orthodontist. He's single. Here's his number."

Violet managed to keep a straight face

until they were out of the train. Then she let out a mighty burst of laughter. It was a release of stress, he knew, but still. He hustled her along faster, tucking her arm under his.

"You enjoyed that, didn't you?" he said as they made their way out of the station.

She nodded. "Oh, yes. Immensely."

He sighed. He could handle being lambasted, if it took her mind off Xavier Beck, bringing back her sparkle if only for a few moments.

"Come on, Vi. Maybe I can redeem myself for my boorish behavior."

"Doubtful," she said, squeezing his hand, "but it will be amusing to see you try."

The apartment building in Manhattan was on the Upper West Side, half a block from Central Park. They'd finished the last leg of the journey in a cab. Rents here were high, and she wondered about Zach's acquaintance. Tidying her hair and straightening her jacket, she worried she looked like a vagrant with her ruined shoe. They'd already gotten stares from the taxi driver, the doorman and the lady waxing the floors, who looked pointedly at Violet's broken heel. They were buzzed through the lobby and up to a third-floor studio apartment.

"Who is Archie Ballentine?" she said.

"Friend of the family. He's at work, but he said to make ourselves at home." Zach used a key to open the door.

"Why do you have a key?"

"Friends, like I said. He's got a key to our place, too."

Must be very good friends, she thought, if he had a key to a cop's house. The interior was small, with a brick wall and hardwood floors. A neatly made queen-size bed opened onto a tiny kitchen. Another door led to the equally tiny bathroom. Zach walked to the windows that looked down onto 82nd Street. He must have been satisfied, since he drew the curtains and went to the bottom drawer of the dresser.

“Here,” he said, handing her a pair of jeans and a T-shirt. “Archie’s sister stays here sometimes and she left some things. Archie said to borrow what you needed and shower and change. Sorry there’s no shoes, though.”

“I’m okay… I…”

Zach’s look went mournful. “Please, Vi. I’ve already been chewed up by two ladies about how I should take better care of my sweetheart. At least allow me to do this and fix you something to eat so I can salvage some shred of dignity.”

“But you’re not my sweetheart, so you’re off the hook.” Not her sweetheart, just a man she trusted with her life, who knew her better and deeper than anyone else on the planet. And why did her stomach go fluttery when she looked at him now, all strong and tender at the same time?

He pushed the bundled clothes at her. “While you shower, I need to make some calls and I'm going to fix you some eggs if there are any."

Her doubt must have shown on her face.

"Why are you giving me that look? I can cook eggs," he said defensively.

"Since when?"

"Since, like, forever."

"Last time you tried to make eggs we had to throw away the pan."

"Aww, go shower, wouldja? I need to recapture some self-esteem. You just wait. The eggs are going to be awe-inspiring. Much better than an orthodontist could make."

Taking the clothes, she squeezed into the bathroom. A narrow stand-up shower was crowded in with a pedestal sink and toilet, but to Violet it was finer than accommodations at the Four Seasons. The hot water rinsed away the grit and grime and she helped herself to a dollop of shampoo. It felt glorious to be clean, and though Archie's sister was a bigger size than Violet, she was grateful for the gentle softness of the borrowed clothes next to her skin. She used her scarf as a makeshift belt to cinch the waist of the jeans.

The mirror cast a sobering reflection back at her that took away some of her contentment. A scrape grazed the cheek that was already bruised from Beck's airport attack and there was another scratch on her forehead. But what Violet was most shocked by was the fear she saw imprinted on her own face.

Where was the independent, self-assured woman she thought she'd been hours before? Now she was nose to nose with someone small and scared, unsure, a woman who'd seen a life snuffed out right next to her. It came back in a horrifying rush. Clinging to the edge of the sink, she searched for strength. An image of Zach rose in her mind. *Zach is here, and he won't let anything happen to me.*

She didn't want to depend on someone

else for her peace of mind. The very idea offended her sensibilities, but nonetheless Zach's presence was the only thing keeping the terror at bay. He was right there, in the kitchen, and his nearness meant comfort and shelter, whether she could admit it or not. Straightening her shoulders, she tucked her hair behind her ears. With her nerves bolstered a little, she pattered out of the bathroom on bare feet to find him before her confidence could evaporate.

The acrid smell of burning eggs tickled her nostrils. She found Zach staring mournfully into a blackened pan at the remnants of what had probably been his attempt at scrambled eggs.

"Oh, dear," she said.

"I don't get it." He shook his head. "I watched a YouTube video. I thought I did everything right."

"It's okay. I wasn't very hungry, anyway."

He heaved out a breath. "You know, I'm beginning to suspect I'm not very good at cooking."

The understatement of the decade. Through sheer force of will, she smothered a smile and a peal of laughter. “You just need more practice.”

“I was trying to get some at the house.” He groaned. “My brothers have started to call me The Incinerator. The only thing I can make is Eddie’s treats and that’s only because Ellie helps me. A six-year-old is a better cook than I am.”

She giggled. “You can’t be good at everything.”

He shoved the pan in the sink, filled it with water, his back to her. Hands braced on the counter, his head dropped. “No, only one thing. I have to be good at being a cop. It’s all I have,” he mumbled to the soapy water.

“You are a great cop.” She sensed the pain and she put her hands on his shoulders, kneading the taut muscles. He relaxed slightly, letting out a deep sigh. Her fingers massaged his neck as if she could ease away his doubt.

"I'm not sure anymore."

The vulnerability jarred her. He'd actually shared the crack in his confidence, a deeply painful thing for him to expose to anyone. "You will catch Beck," she said firmly, pressing her cheek hard to his spine. "And you will find the man who murdered Jordy and you will experience joy again, just like God wants."

He was silent for a long moment and then he turned around to face her. His eyes were thoughtful, so blue, exquisitely earnest. "Do you really still believe in me like that, Vi?"

"I really do."

"Why?" It came out as the softest whisper.

"Because I trust you, just like I did when I climbed the tree. You wouldn't let me fall then and you won't now. Jordy trusted you and you won't let him down, either."

His face was close to hers, his breath and body warm. He brushed a thumb along her cheek.

"I know you're scared," he said.

"Not me."

His touch was as gentle as the smile playing across his lips. "You're lying, Vi."

Her lip trembled. "Maybe pretending, just a little." His caress continued to connect her to him, to make a bridge past the fear to a new place that she hadn't been before.

And then his mouth was on hers and her whole world grew fuzzy around the edges. Sparks circled and danced in her spirit like fireflies on a warm spring night. He stopped for a moment, looking at her in wonder, and then he leaned in for another kiss.

THIRTEEN

Zach pressed his mouth to hers and reveled in the explosion of comfort that flooded over him. It felt like coming home. He buried his hand in her hair and held her there, her lips soft as satin. His brain could not keep up with the confusion he felt at kissing the woman who was supposed to be his friend only. Somehow with his kiss he had eased them into a new wild and thrilling territory. *This is a bad idea*, his brain blared at him.

So he stopped listening to his brain and kissed her again, letting his heart guide him toward what it wanted. When they were both breathless, she eased away a fraction, and he looked in disbelief at the brown eyes that stared from under a curtain of long lashes, reflecting his own surprise back at him. His face looked like that of a man in love.

"Zach..." she breathed.

Then the door opened and he shoved her behind him, grabbing his gun and charging the front door.

Archie Ballentine jerked to a halt with a grocery bag in one arm. He was a short plug of a man, close to seventy now, with a cap of snowy hair and a suit, custom-made, to go with his leather wing tips. "Hello, Zach. I'd raise my hands and surrender, but I don't want to drop the groceries."

Zach exhaled and holstered his weapon. "I thought you were working."

"Closed the deal early."

"You should have texted me. I could have shot you."

"I did text you." His brow hitched a fraction as he scanned Violet's face and then Zach's. "You were distracted, I guess..."

Archie had always had the uncanny ability to read Zach like a book. It didn't help that Zach's breathing was still erratic and his heart was thumping like Eddie's tail after a bust. He cleared his throat, hoping he did not still look like a lovesick puppy. "I'm sorry. Very glad to see you, we both are. Sure do appreciate your help, Archie."

"Figured you might want some food for the lady." He gave the bag to Zach along with a hug, and extended his palm to Violet.

"Vi, this is Archie Ballentine." The mundane introduction seemed ridiculous to Zach, when he was still reeling from kissing Violet. He could not tell from her face how the kiss had affected her, except for a slight petal-pink blush staining her cheeks. Ten minutes before, he would never have believed he'd have kissed Violet Griffin, not like that, anyway.

"Nice to meet you," she said. "Thank you for letting me come here."

"Sure," Archie said. "When a Jameson

says he needs something, the answer is always yes. This time, however, I am a little lacking in details."

"I'll fill you in." Zach deposited the groceries on the kitchen counter as he talked. He started with the airport incident and quickly outlined events that led to his desperate text to Archie on the subway ride from Queens.

Archie nodded. "So this Xavier Beck's at large. Is he the big boss or is there someone else?"

"Bill hinted there was a bigger guy behind it all." He caught Violet's wince at the mention of her deceased boss. "I, uh… It's been a traumatic couple of hours."

Archie nodded thoughtfully. "I think I got it. What's the game plan?"

"Keep Vi here tonight, if that's okay."

Violet started to object, but Zach shook her off. "Beck's going to stick around. I want you here for a while to give our guys a chance to catch him and to set up a tighter watch schedule at your house. He's been seen by a ton of people and the cops are all over, so he won't be able to remain long out in the open. It's safer for you to stay here tonight."

She slid a look at Archie. "Is it fair to involve Mr. Ballentine in a dangerous situation?"

"Call me Archie," he said. "And offering up my apartment is a no-brainer. As far as danger goes..." He shrugged. "I can take care of myself."

"That's for sure. Always land on your feet somehow," Zach said with a laugh. "And as I recall you've beaten Carter in a judo match a time or two."

Archie grinned. "Yes, I have. More than a time or two in my younger days. His hip throw was terrible back then. Couldn't knock over a toddler."

Zach grinned. "Still can't."

"When did you two meet?" Violet asked.

Zach leaned on the kitchen counter. "Jordy

and I arrested him." They both chuckled at the look of shock on Violet's face.

"All right, Miss Violet," Archie said. "Sit down at the table, if you're still willing now that you know I'm a reformed felon. I brought sandwiches because The Incinerator here can't boil water without setting something on fire."

Zach groaned. "You've been talking to my brothers."

"I check in when I can. Since my apartment smells like burned eggs, I assume you haven't changed your ways. Sit down, both of you, and I'll explain before we get ourselves a game plan." Archie passed out pastrami sandwiches and cans of soda.

Zach realized for the first time that he was starving. He'd missed both breakfast and lunch and it was well on toward the dinner hour. He ate hungrily, while Violet only managed a few bites.

"Eat, Vi," he said. "You've got to get some food down."

“That’s what I’ve been telling you for the past two months,” she said, sampling a small bite.

“I’m eating. Your turn.” He wiped his mouth. “Archie was involved in a little fake taxi scam, about fifteen years ago.”

“Not little,” he said, chin up. “I made six grand a week as a cabbie for City Wheels Rides, the best company in all of New York City.”

Zach shook his head. “Only there was no City Wheels Rides company, just a mock-up sticker on the door of his sedan, and a fake meter in the front seat.”

“Hey, the important thing was I always delivered people on time and many would request me specifically. I was their favorite driver and they’d give me Christmas gifts, family photos, even a fruit basket once. ‘Give us Archie,’ they all cried. I was the people’s choice.”

“Right up until the day we arrested you with your fake permits, license and forged insurance papers.”

Archie waved a hand. "Small potatoes when you should have been chasing down real criminals. Anyway, Jordan said I was the most charismatic crook he ever busted, and he told me I should stop dithering around, go straight and get into business. I took his advice, got my license to sell real estate and now I'm doing great. All because of Jordy. Man, that guy even prayed for me, can you believe that? A cop praying for a crook he busted?"

Zach cleared a lump from his throat. "Yeah. Jordy had a way of seeing the good in people."

"Yes, he did." Archie sighed. "Boy, do I miss him."

Zach swallowed hard. "Me, too."

"Me, three," Violet added. The moment lingered there a while, and Zach thought about what Violet had said before he kissed her.

And you will find the man who murdered Jordy and you will experience joy again, just like God wants. Strange. He'd spent the past two months figuring God had to be against him, but here, crowded around this table with Violet and Archie, he had a sense that his brother was close again, cheering him on. And he'd certainly felt something very akin to joy when he'd kissed Violet in the kitchen. The warm feeling ebbed away as reality intruded.

Jordy's killer was out there, at large, just like Xavier Beck, waiting to rob him of someone else he cared about…and loved?

Loved? Across the table, Violet pushed her plate away. Her hair was curling as it dried; he remembered the feel of it in his fingers, heavy and light at the same time. Loved…as a friend, he told himself. He'd been caught up in the moment, the emotional cascade, same as Violet. He had tugged her out onto the unfamiliar territory, testing the boundaries of a friendship he was not prepared to lose. Archie had come through the door at exactly the right moment to save him from ruining everything. She was a friend, one he had to save, and he had work to do.

Clearing his throat, he rose from the table. "I've arranged for a plainclothes detective to watch the place while I'm gone."

"I can handle it," Archie said.

"I don't doubt it, but someone eyeballing the street won't hurt."

Violet followed him to the door. "Where are you going?"

"Noah called me about a possible lead while you were showering and I was destroying the eggs. There's a furniture store near the airport that might be a front for moving drugs. Beck was spotted there earlier this afternoon. Eddie and I are going in undercover and I need to work out the details. Plus, I'm going to check every local health-care clinic and see if a guy matching Beck's description checked in since I got him with a bullet across his shoulder."

Violet played with her paper napkin uncertainly.

Archie clapped him on the back. "All right. Watch your back and I'll watch Violet's." He carried the remaining groceries to the tiny fridge and began to unload them. Zach pulled on his jacket and headed to the door, Violet following. He stepped out into the hallway and she lingered on the threshold, looking down at her bare feet, the toenails painted a delicate pink. He could picture her curled up on her apartment sofa, surrounded by her home decorating magazines and shoe catalogs, stroking paint onto her tiny nails. It was such a girly image, so far from the businesslike woman he thought he knew inside and out. Suddenly, his thinking skills seemed to dry up in one swift stroke as the silence grew awkward between them and they both stared at the floor.

"You have cute toes," he blurted, ruing the statement as soon as it popped out of his mouth. *Smooth, Zach.*

"Thanks for noticing."

"Well, I mean, I guess I haven't seen them in a while...your toes. I just didn't realize they were, you know, cute and stuff, with the paint. So, uh, what color is that, anyway?" Why would his mouth not stop spitting out stupidity?

"Carnation Kisses."

"Ah. Er, that's nice. I mean, it looks nice."

She nodded.

More awkward silence.

"I…" They both said at once.

"I'm sorry," he said, overriding her. "About back there in the kitchen. I got caught up in everything and it just kind of happened." He scrubbed a hand over his scalp. "I shouldn't have kissed you."

She shrugged, gave him a valiant smile. "No harm, no foul."

"What I'm trying to say is, I wouldn't want to do anything to mess up our friendship."

"You didn't. You'll always be my trusty sidekick."

Relief flooded through him in a cooling tide. The ship was upright again, sailing back on the proper course. She was still his friend, his best friend. "Right." He jammed on the baseball cap. "Okay, then. I'll see if I can get your purse back, too, and your phone."

"Okay."

"So, in the meantime, Archie can reach me if you need anything. Text, or call, anytime."

"I will. Be careful, Zach."

He nodded. Then there seemed to be nothing else to say, so he walked away and she locked the door behind him.

After forty-five minutes of small talk, helping Archie unpack the groceries and scrubbing out the burned egg pan, Violet washed her face in the bathroom again and summoned up the courage she needed. She borrowed Archie's phone to call her parents. Archie excused himself to go to the lobby and retrieve his mail. She suspected he was gifting her some privacy. As the quiet of the apartment closed in around her, a trembling started up in her belly. The emptiness spread and invaded until she was half-frantic. Her fingers were clumsy on the buttons.

"Hello, Daddy, it's Violet." She got the words out, barely, before her father started in.

"Violet, this has gone too far," he said, his voice cracking with anger and fear. "We heard about the shooting. I can't stand it. No more airport job, do you hear? You have to quit. Working for that crooked boss almost got you killed."

And whoever Bill was working for had gotten him killed. Again, the pop of the gun played in her memory, the sound of him falling to the sidewalk, his life stripped away in one cruel moment. She wanted to explain to her father what had happened with Bill, that he wasn't a bad person, just a father who'd made a grievous choice, a choice that turned out to be fatal. The words would not come. She was simply too exhausted to go into it. Instead, she heaved out a breath and swallowed. "I will see if I can find work at another airport, but for now I'm taking a leave of absence." It was a defeat. Her job, her life, everything was topsy-turvy because of what she had seen for a split second in a bad man's suitcase. How utterly ridiculous, how completely unjust.

"Good," her mother said from the other line. "You'll stay with us? Until this madman is caught? The puppy is driving me crazy. He chewed up the sofa pillows today and there is not one shrub still standing in the yard."

Violet wished Latte was there right now for her to cuddle, the soft, warm companion who would lick her chin and flop over for tummy scratches. "Yes, Mom. I will come home as soon as Zach lets me," she squeezed out.

"I'm so glad Zach was there with you." Her father's breath sounded hard and erratic over the phone. “I don’t even want to think about what could have happened.”

“Yes,” she said quietly. “I… I wouldn’t have lived through it, probably.” Undoubtedly. Beck’s second bullet would have been for her. The tremors grew stronger until she had to grip the phone with two hands.

“Where are you now?” her mother asked.

“With a friend of the Jamesons’. I’ll be home soon, as soon as I can. There will most likely be a memorial service for Bill. I should help with the plans.”

“Absolutely not,” her father snapped. “You are to have nothing more to do with Bill Oscar, do you hear me?”

“He can’t cause any more trouble now, Daddy.” Violet gulped back a sob. “He’s dead.”

Her father’s tone gentled. “Yes, I… I’m sorry, sweet pea. This is terrible on you, and I’m not helping. We can talk about all this tomorrow. I’d rather you were home right now, but if Zach says this is best, then I’ll go along with it. You try to get some rest, okay? We love you."

"Yes," her mother echoed quietly. "We do."

She considered the amazing strength of Barbara Griffin. Having lost her only son and almost her daughter, as well, her mother remained composed, a magnificent courage she'd never appreciated fully until that moment. It made her hold the unraveling threads of her self-control long enough to say goodbye.

She barely managed to disconnect before the tears came, racking sobs and shudders. She wished she were in her own apartment where she could wail in private. Hunched into a ball on the futon with her arms around her knees, she tried to smother her outpouring. She didn't realize Archie had returned until he softly cleared his throat. There was no place to hide her condition, not in a studio apartment. Without a word, he handed her a box of tissues and led her to the bed.

"Lie down, Miss Violet. Rest awhile."

"I'm sorry," she said. "I'm not usually like this. I don't know what's wrong with me."

"You've experienced the worst the world has to offer," he said. "That's what's wrong. Time to allow yourself to be taken care of. Trust an old coot on this. Nap time for Violet."

In a fog, she allowed him to tuck the blankets around her. "But…it's your bed."

"Like I told Zach, I'm apartment-sitting for my friend next door. I'll crash on his couch after I do some work, but I'll come check on you. You sleep. I'll work. Zach will find the bad guy. Everyone's got their job, you see?"

She prayed that it would happen just like Archie said.

"Oh, and here's something that might cheer you. Zach brought this up for you while you were in the bathroom." He handed her a white box. Inside were a pair of soft leather flats with chic silver buckles, size six, and a note.

Figured you needed some workable shoes. I called the shoe store and the owner sent these over. I got the size off your busted one. Hope they fit. —Z

"He bought me shoes," she said, dumbly.

"Yes, he did. That Zach is something. Not every man has the chutzpah to tackle shoe purchasing. Heart of a lion."

She smiled, her throat suddenly thickened, heart beating fast at the memory of their kiss. What had that kiss done to her? That one moment seemed to have altered the pathways of her emotions, pathways she'd worked very hard to straighten out.

I wouldn't want to do anything to mess up our friendship.

Friendship was all it was, was all it could ever be, though her heart wanted something else altogether. She'd been vulnerable, and that attracted him for a moment, because he was a fixer, but that wasn't her. Violet Griffin was not needy, not weak and not going to offer her heart to a man who did not want her that way. If Zach broke her heart, she knew it would be a fatal blow.

Tears blurred her vision as she laid the shoes in their box carefully on the bed beside her, tucking the tissue paper around them before she closed her eyes.

FOURTEEN

The scent of coffee brought Zach out of his sprawling slumber the next morning. He cracked open a bleary eye to see a set of hairy knuckles waving a steaming mug next to his nose. Jerking upright and knocking over a pencil cup in the process, he realized he'd been sleeping on top of his desk in the K-9 office headquarters. Bunkered in his cubicle on the ground floor of the three-story building, he'd spent the night calling health clinics. The process took longer than it should have thanks to endless holds and his own fumbling, but Zach was used to that.

"Up and at 'em, sunshine," his brother Carter said, sliding the mug closer. Zach groaned, tried to stretch the stiffness out of his kinked neck and shake away the headache that had settled in his temples. Retrieving the scattered pencils, he jammed them back into the cup. Frosty regarded him with amused interest from his cushion in the corner. Zach slugged down some coffee too fast, burning his mouth. Wincing, he spilled some on his shirtfront.

"This stuff's the temperature of lava," he complained.

"The general consensus of the NYPD is that coffee is best served hot." Carter chuckled. "You look like something the dogs dug up in the park."

"You're hilarious."

"I know. Find out anything pulling an all-nighter?"

"No. No one with Beck's description sought medical help anywhere that I can find."

"Yeah, that was a long shot, anyway. He probably patched himself up. Found his bike tossed in a parking lot. Dusting it for prints and all that good stuff so we're in waiting mode, but we're pretty sure it's his."

"All right." Zach sucked down more coffee, slower this time, letting the caffeine bring him back to life. It wasn't nearly as good as Violet's. He hoped she'd been able to get some rest and that she'd liked his shoe gift. Picturing her opening them gave him a warm sensation. *Head in the game, Zach.* "Give me what you have on the furniture store. My gut says it's a front to move drugs and Beck's gotta be connected somehow. Fill me in."

"No."

Zach stared. "Whaddya mean?"

"I mean no, as in no way, I'm not going to give you any info on that."

Zach caught the gleam of stubborn enjoyment in Carter's expression. "Why not?" he asked slowly.

Carter shrugged. "We got eyes on the store. Nothing spicy so far, just normal everyday capitalism at work. Maybe when you take Eddie in you'll know more, but Noah said that's not going to happen until you come home and sleep for four hours, so he told me to give you precisely zero info about the location or stakeout details."

Zach gaped. "That's insane."

"Four hours, that's two hundred forty minutes."

He got to his feet and stalked from behind the desk and followed Carter out of his cubicle. "Carter, quit playing around."

"Not my call. Noah's the chief."

"But enforced nap time? I'm not a toddler."

"Really? 'Cause I think you drooled on your desk."

At his full height, Zach was a shade taller than his brother and he tried to take advantage. "You're gonna tell me right now what I want to know."

"I don't think so."

He glared at Carter. "The store may prove

to be a connection to Beck. It's our only lead right now. Vi was shot at, almost killed by this creep yesterday after he murdered her boss, or hadn't you heard about that?"

"I'm well aware, but Noah said you're not going to do her or anyone any good if you don't sleep. He's already talked to Archie, and Violet is just fine. As a matter of fact, Luke delivered her purse and cell phone and some take-out Chinese in an unmarked car. Archie picked it up and brought it to her." He grinned. "I think it's okay to disclose it was hot and sour soup and egg rolls. We'll bring her home later this afternoon."

"I'm not going to lie around and have nappy time while we've got two cases going cold." It came out louder than he'd meant.

"Yes, you are. It's a DO."

"I don't care if it's a direct order or not. You're gonna spit out whatever we've got on the furniture store right now."

"Actually," Carter said calmly, "I'm not."

They spent a long moment in a stare

down, Jameson to Jameson. After ten seconds he knew he wasn't going to win. He might be able to beat Carter in a judo match, but his brother matched him inch for inch in toughness and determination.

"What about Jordy?" Zach demanded, hands on hips. "Do I get a status report on that at least, or do I have to nap first?"

Carter mimed zipping his lips and throwing away the key.

Zach felt like growling and putting his brother in a headlock. "You know I can take you, right?"

"In your dreams. I beat you at the hoops in our last game and if that's not enough, my dog is way tougher than your dog."

"Carter..."

"Go home, little brother, and get some sleep. If you need me to come sing you a lullaby and tuck you in, let me know." Carter turned on his heel and left Zach fuming. Frosty tossed one glance at Zach before they cleared the room that might as well have been, "Yeah, I am tougher than your measly beagle and don't you forget it."

And then he was left standing there, helpless, like a kid lost at the mall. He had half a mind to go get Eddie and storm the furniture store by himself, but he would not do that to Noah, just as he would not ever have defied Jordy's direct order.

He stared at Brianne and Gavin, who were peeking around their cubicle walls.

"And I don't suppose either of you two are going to tell me anything?"

Brianne ignored him completely, studiously avoiding eye contact, vanishing again behind her cubicle walls. Gavin gave him a sympathetic half smile, which stung worse than being ignored. It wouldn't do any good to pester any of the other K-9 unit members, either, as he was sure Noah had given his directive to all of them. Brianne and Gavin had heard every embarrassing word, of course, adding to his humiliation of being ordered to bed like a misbehaving child.

He stalked to his car, grateful that a fellow cop had driven it back from Astoria. Exceeding the speed limit and bristling with anger all the way home, he found the place deserted. Even Ellie and the puppies were gone away, getting their next vet checkup. They were probably all giving him a wide berth, knowing how he'd react to Noah's order. The whole clan was in on it, he was sure. Too angry to sleep, he took a shower, shaved, dressed and ate a container of yogurt without tasting it, followed by a peanut butter and jelly sandwich. In the process of cleaning up, he knocked a mug off the table and it smashed into three neat pieces on the kitchen tile.

Just great. He knew Violet would have laughed in that throaty way that never failed to make him join in. After he cleaned up the shards of porcelain, he flopped on his bed, overwhelmed by the irresistible urge to phone her.

But there was that kiss…and those feelings…and the stomach-dropping roller-coaster sensation when he recalled it all and the way he was having a harder and harder time thinking of her merely as a friend. Instead, he went out and retrieved Eddie and let him up on the sofa, even though they'd agreed as a family that the furniture was solely for people. "You won't tell, will you?"

Eddie wagged his tail and curled up with Zach on the couch. Again, Zach craved to hear Violet's voice.

Don't, he told himself. Not when he could still feel the sparks of their unexpected kiss. But that was behind them, a moment of insanity. It wasn't love, right? It was okay to phone a friend, wasn't it? Probably not a good idea at this juncture, but his disobedient fingers dialed anyway. She picked up on the first ring.

"Hi," he said. "Glad you got your cell phone back."

"Hi, yourself. Are you okay?"

"Yeah, just dropped a coffee mug on the

kitchen floor, but fortunately, there's no one here to witness it."

She laughed, and it was a sound sweeter than the swish of a three-point shot from half-court. If a broken mug would ease her pain, he'd smash a million of them.

"That's pretty typical," she said. "At least it was only one. Why do you sound irritated?"

How could she tell over the phone? "I'm on enforced nap time, if you can believe it. Noah's got this ridiculous notion that I need rest."

"Because you pulled an all-nighter in your office?"

His jaw dropped. "How did you know that?"

"Because I know you."

Yes, she did. Better than anyone in the world. She knew him to the core, but she could not know the strange river of emotions that had begun to run through him when he thought about her. At least he hoped not.

Get it together, Zach. "Yeah, well, anyway, it's humiliating, and I don't appreciate being double-teamed by my brothers."

"Do you need me to state the obvious?"

"What?"

"That Noah loves you." She paused. "That he's taking care of you the only way he knows how."

"I can take care of myself," he said hotly, but her words quenched the flame of his anger and he sighed.

"He lost a brother, too, Zach," she said quietly. "Caring for you could be helping him heal."

Helping Noah heal? He didn't know what to say to that. It had never occurred to him that accepting coddling would help anyone else. Yet hadn't it made him feel like a superhero to arrange for shoes for Vi? And hadn't he desperately wanted to cook those eggs for her? But that wasn't coddling, just...friendliness. "I don't need any hand-holding from him," he said finally.

"Or anyone else."

"Hey, you're a fine one to talk, Miss Independence."

"Touché." She was quiet a moment. "How about a deal?"

"What deal?"

"When this…situation is all over and Beck is caught, we'll agree to let each other help with one thing."

"One thing? Like what?"

"Like… I can help you learn to scramble an egg."

"I don't need help. I just had a bad day. I'm okay at that."

"No, you're not."

"I'm insulted."

"You just need a little tweak, that's all. Five minutes of help and you'll be a pro."

He chuckled. "I'd like to see that on my apron instead of The Incinerator. All right. What do I have to help you with?"

"Perfecting a new recipe for lemon meringue pie. I've wanted to make it for my mom's birthday, and I just can't get it right. So far I've been defeated every time."

He laughed at that one. "It's more than likely going to be counterproductive to have me in the kitchen for pie building when I need a tutorial to scramble an egg."

"I just need a sous-chef and someone to stir the hot custard while I whisk in the eggs. We'll keep the fire extinguisher handy. Do we have a deal or not, Jameson?"

He sighed, a smile curving his lips as he thought about his wheeling, dealing, don't-take-no-for-an-answer Violet. As if he had the power to say no to her. "Okay. Deal."

"Excellent. I will hold you to the bargain."

"Of that, I'm certain."

Her giggle was girlish, but it died away quickly. "Um, thank you for the shoes."

"Do they fit?"

"Perfectly."

"Do you like them?"

"So much."

So much. The pleasure at having made

her happy was as restorative as a full night's rest. "Good. I don't know the first thing about women's shoes." He held the phone tighter to his ear. "How are you doing, Vi? Really?"

"I slept a little."

"That isn't what I meant."

"I'm okay," she said, too quickly. "I talked to Bill's wife on the phone. That was… hard."

Excruciating, he imagined.

She continued. "I want to go home and help with Latte and the diner. When will I be allowed to?"

"Soon."

"Not soon enough. I… I need to be busy."

It was an admission that she would never have made before, a fragile offering, it seemed to him. Picturing her there, holding the phone, made him desire nothing more than to wrap her in a hug, to feel the tickle of her hair under his chin. His pulse seemed to surge into a higher rhythm.

He shifted on the sofa and added his own. "Yeah, I feel the same way. Work is the only thing that helps."

"And prayer."

Rage and prayer were not compatible. Though the rage over his brother's death had taken a back burner the past week to worrying over Vi, he did not think it would ever abate completely. It left him blind and caught in a place he did not want to be. "I can't pray right now, so maybe you can do it for us both." He'd asked her for prayer. Had it really come out of his mouth? There was some relief in it and he knew it was a step, tiny and faltering, toward healing.

"I can, and I do, every day." Her voice cracked but she quickly composed herself and added brightly, "So go get that nap, would you? And you'd better make sure Eddie is off the sofa before the family comes home."

"How did you know…?"

She laughed. "Like I said, I know you, Zach Jameson, so get some sleep."

"Yes, ma'am," he said.

FIFTEEN

The operation at the furniture store had to be postponed until afternoon, since the place was unexpectedly shut Saturday morning. "Closed until three for a family emergency," the sign taped to the door stated. Zach wondered if the family emergency had something to do with Beck's crime spree or the drug seizure at Victor's apartment, but there was no choice but to wait for afternoon to roll around. At least Violet was back, with a plainclothes cop watching her at all times plus a diner full of officers at any given moment. Beck was insane, but Zach did not think he would come after Violet with so much law enforcement around.

Then again, he'd been wrong before about Beck's boldness.

As the hours ticked away, he drove his family nuts with his incessant motion, shooting hoops, running on the treadmill, shuffling and reshuffling papers, pacing while he checked his cell phone.

Ellie approached him. "Do you want to go outside and play ball, Uncle Zach?"

He sighed. "Your father put you up to this, didn't he?"

"Yes. He told me you need someone to play with."

He laughed and tugged her pigtail. "It's okay, squirt. You don't have to babysit me."

"I like to babysit you," she said. "You're fun to play with, and you let me have ice cream. You know where Uncle Jordy hides the treats." She frowned. "I mean, where he hid them."

She stuck a finger in her mouth. He sank to one knee. "Do you feel sad right now, Ellie?"

She nodded, not looking at him.

"It's okay," he said. "It's okay to feel that way."

She sniffed and looked at him. "Do you feel sad, too? About Uncle Jordy going to Heaven?"

He fought for control. What was the right thing to say to a child when he couldn't even comfort himself? "I'm glad Uncle Jordy's in Heaven now, but I sure do feel sad that he can't be here with us."

"Do you cry sometimes?"

"Yes, I do."

"Me, too." She was thoughtful for a moment. "He was real good at playing ball."

"Yeah, the best." He waited for the razor-edged pain in his throat to subside enough for him to talk. "Your idea was super. Let's go play some catch and find the ice cream. I think there's still some in the freezer. Your uncle Jordy would want us to have some, wouldn't he?"

He'd won a smile on that precious face.

Thank You, God. Thanking God? Why should he do that? But looking into his niece's eyes, how could he not? Jordy was gone but there was love here, still here, right before his eyes. How could he feel both love and agony at the same time? Confused, he followed her through the sliding door.

He spent some time playing in the backyard with Ellie and ate frozen ice cream treats with her. He thought Violet might have been proud of him for the way he'd handled things. It surprised him how much he hoped she would be.

Finally, three o'clock rolled around and he clipped on Eddie's civilian leash and made sure his radio transmitter was functioning. Noah and Carter and two other cops were in position as backup, monitoring from their unmarked vehicles parked in the vicinity of the furniture store.

Zach wore jeans and a baggy sweatshirt to hide the transmitter taped to his side, and his gun. If Beck was inside, he'd be recognized immediately, but so far there had been no sign of the guy. He was pleased to see that Eddie was his usual easygoing self. The dog had been upset at being separated from Zach at the shooting scene and at being brought home by someone other than Zach, and he'd hoped their couch time was enough to ease his mind. Zach could always tell when Eddie was agitated because the dog would chew relentlessly on the door to his kennel. For all his amazing law-enforcement capabilities, Eddie was a sensitive dog who had been treated cruelly in his puppy years.

While they had waited for the hours to slip by, Zach had spent a little extra time playing ball with Eddie and brushing his coat until the dog's eyes rolled with satisfaction, which restored him to normal. Now he was relaxed and eager to see what the next mission would dole out.

"All right, buddy. Here we go." Zach

walked Eddie down the street and into the furniture store.

"Sir," a red-shirted man said right away. He was thin, so thin his polo shirt hung loose on his lanky frame. His name tag read Hugo. "I'm sorry, but we don't allow dogs in here," Hugo said.

Zach offered a smile. "It will only take a few minutes. Eddie is really well trained."

The man looked doubtful.

"I mean, I don't shop anywhere without my dog, and I really need to make a purchase quick."

"Well..." Hugo said. His eyes rolled in thought as he weighed the cost of breaking the rules against a potential lost commission.

"It's just that I really need a new sofa because Eddie here likes to chew, and he mangled mine. I don't have much time to find one. I was really hoping to make a purchase today."

Zach could see Hugo's eyes light up at the

prospect of a quick sale. Decision made. "I guess it's all right, as long as he doesn't chew any of these sofas."

Zach made small talk, asked some questions and waited for his opportunity. When Hugo went to answer the phone, Zach bent down and patted Eddie. "Find the drugs, boy."

Then he and Eddie wandered through the displayed furniture groupings. Eddie was uninterested until they made their way closer to the back of the store, crowded with massive wardrobes, towering bookshelves and coffee tables scattered about. Eddie began to tug at the leash. Zach feigned interest in the table with oak leaves carved into the wooden legs on which Eddie was fixated.

The salesman hurried over.

"You know," Zach said. "This table would look great in my den. How much are you asking for it?"

Hugo fiddled with his pen. "I'm very sorry, sir. That piece has been purchased."

"I don't see a sold sign anywhere on it."

"An oversight on our part. It was sold a few minutes ago."

Zach noticed a bead of sweat trickle down the man's temple. "Really? I thought you just opened up shop for the day."

"Uh, well, perhaps it was yesterday, but it's sold, for sure."

Zach frowned. "But I really like this table." Eddie nosed excitedly at one of the wooden legs. "My dog does, too."

Hugo's manner became even sunnier. "We have some similar pieces that I am certain you'll like. Or I'm happy to show you a catalog. We can even have custom pieces made with enough lead time."

"Naw, it has to be this table," Zach pressed. "I'll offer more than your current buyer."

Now the man was swallowing hard, his Adam's apple bobbing up and down. Another man appeared, black-haired and clean-shaven, wearing a nice suit. He must have been listening to the conversation from the back room. His arms were muscled under the sleeves, neck thick, like he'd seen the inside of a boxing ring a time or two. Zach eased back on his feet just enough, just in case.

"Sir," the burly guy said. "I'm sorry. It would be unethical for us to resell this table to you when it's already been spoken for. I'm sure you understand." His jacket was buttoned and Zach would not have been surprised to know he had a gun hidden underneath. Casually, Zach loosened his hold on the leash, ready in case he needed to draw his own weapon. Adrenaline began to pump through his veins, but he kept his demeanor calm, relaxed. He flashed a smile. "Oh, come on. I know there has to be something you can do. Everyone has a price." Eddie tried to sniff around the big guy's legs, to get at the table behind him.

"No," the jacketed guy said coldly. "But if there's nothing else you're interested in, I'll have to ask you to leave. We don't allow animals in our store."

Eddie was oblivious to the conversation. He whined, circled three times and sat, staring at Zach.

I know, buddy. Play it cool.

Zach feigned insult. "Fine. If I can't have the table, I don't want a sofa, either. I'll take my business elsewhere. Plenty of other shops around."

"Very sorry we couldn't help you. Have a good day, sir," the nervous salesperson called as Zach left. The other man did not say a word, but Zach could feel a cold stare boring into his back.

As they headed for the entrance, Eddie whined and tugged at the leash, loath to leave his find. By sheer force of will, Zach got him out of the store and radioed Noah.

"Did you copy that? Eddie alerted."

"We're already processing a search warrant. We'll have it here within the hour," Noah said.

"Back door?"

"Covered. Carter's there with Frosty, keeping watch. We'll eyeball the front. Nothing's gonna leave that place without us knowing."

Zach's nerves were still zinging as he guided Eddie to a quiet spot on the side-walk and gave him a treat. Eddie accepted his prize, dropping it on the sidewalk to lick it properly before he chewed. "You did a good job, baby. We'll make the bust. Just gotta wait a while." He got a tail wag and a yip in reply.

He walked Eddie around the block, where he found Carter and Frosty in Carter's car. Without asking, he got in the front, Eddie scrambling onto his lap. Frosty barked.

"Deal with it, dog," Zach said.

Carter grinned. "Still crabby that we cut you out of the action for a while?"

"Crabby doesn't begin to describe it."

"Sorry, man."

"But not too sorry, right?"

"Well, it was fun to mess with you, I'll admit."

Carter straightened as a door opened in the back of the furniture store. "Who's that?"

Exiting the store from the rear was a figure muffled in a coat and knit cap. Zach didn't have to see the face to know the guy. "It's Victor Jones, the guy we got on airport security camera. Bill got him through security a couple of days before the thing went down with Beck. He must have been inside the store somewhere. They figured out what was going down and they're using him to move the drugs before we execute the search warrant."

Jones looked up, saw Carter and Zach staring at him and took off, sprinting down the alley between the furniture store and the warehouse to the rear. Carter called for backup and turned to Zach. "Frosty can run him down. Cut him off at the end of the alley." He leaped from the car and took off on foot, Frosty galloping along beside him.

Zach raced around to the driver's seat, slammed Carter's vehicle into gear and burned out of the parking place, sirens wailing, until he reached the other end of the alley. Braking hard, he lurched the car to a stop. Leaving Eddie inside, he pulled his weapon and charged into the alley. He surged forward, avoiding the patches slick with oil, his nerves electric with anticipation.

We got him. This time, we really got him.

Moments later he met his brother and Frosty coming from the other direction.

"Where is he?" Zach all but shouted.

Carter was breathing hard. "Dunno. He should have exited this way."

They about-faced and Frosty nosed a metal door they had not noticed before.

"Some dog," Zach groaned. "Why didn't he alert earlier?"

"He's a transit dog, not a tracking dog," Carter snapped. They counted to three and burst through the door into an abandoned warehouse, guns drawn. One look at the cavernous empty space filled them in.

Zach slammed a fist against his thigh with frustration. "He got out. Slipped through the front. They've rehearsed it before, no doubt."

"And he took the stash with him, neat as you please."

Zach could have spit nails, but he radioed in Jones's last known position, anyway.

"Our search warrant is gonna get us a big fat zero," Carter said. "Furniture store's gonna be clean as a whistle."

Another lead lost. Another chance to save Violet from harm slipped away.

From the police car, Eddie let out a heart-rending howl.

He felt like doing the same.

Violet was relieved when Zach, Carter and Noah made their way into the diner. It was past their usual dinner hour and Violet was growing worried. One glance at their expressions as they led the dogs to the screened patio area told her everything. The furniture store had been a bust. Xavier Beck was more than likely still on the loose, too, judging from their slumped shoulders. She fought back a chill that rippled over her skin.

Feed them. Wordlessly, she poured bowls of clam chowder and carried them to the men. “Hard day? You must be hungry. Chowder’s good.”

Zach looked so downcast, she longed to put her arms around his neck and whisper comfort, but instead, she tried for a bright smile. “Saturday special is coming, fried chicken.”

Zach shook his head. “Jones slipped between our fingers and we got nothing from the furniture store. Whatever they had in there was long gone. No leads on Beck, either. We got zero out of today, absolutely nothing.”

“Not nothing,” Noah said, checking his phone.

“What?” Zach pushed his soup away.

"Did we get Beck? Victor Jones? Please tell me some good news."

"Okay, here it is, but I'm not sure it qualifies as good. I won't sugarcoat it." Noah blinked as if fighting for control. "We've expected it, so it won't be a surprise to anyone here." He cleared his throat. "Final autopsy reports are in. Jordan died of a massive heart attack due to a cocaine overdose. It was administered via an injection into his upper arm. It wasn't a finesse job, enough to convince the coroner it wasn't self-inflicted. There was no evidence of old tracks, of course."

"We've been telling them that from the beginning," Carter said. "No way was Jordy a user."

Noah raised a palm. "Everyone in the department knew that, but the ME had to rule it out. Her official finding is the death is the result of foul play."

The room fell into a profound silence so

deep that Violet could hear the water dripping in the sink.

"It's not really news, I guess," Noah said. "Just confirming what we already believed, that Jordy didn't kill himself, but now it's official enough that reporters might stop hounding us about it."

Zach's face was stark, pulled taut with extreme emotion. "No, they'll start hounding us about what we've done to catch the killer and we have nothing to say, no progress to report. It's a sizzling story, isn't it? Someone went to great lengths to make his death look like suicide and we have absolutely no idea who that someone is."

Luke Hathaway cleared his throat. "The department is working the case."

"Not hard enough or fast enough," Zach snapped.

"They have good cops on it, Zach," Brianne Hayes said. "They're doing their best and you know it."

"We should be the ones working this case,

the K-9 unit. The investigators spent too much time looking at Claude Jenks, but we know he didn't kill Jordy. We've suspected that from the beginning since Sophie caught him planting the suicide note."

"They had to be thorough. It can't be our investigation. We're too close to it," Finn Gallagher said gently. "Protocols are in place for a reason."

Zach slammed out of his chair. "I don't care about protocols, Finn. My brother was murdered, leaving a wife and child behind, and I did nothing to prevent it." His voice shook. "I'm sure as shooting not going to do nothing to solve it."

"We have to be patient," Noah said, a warning in his tone.

"No, we don't," Zach spat.

The cops looked at each other helplessly as Zach stalked into the screened room and called sharply for Eddie. The expression in his eyes, the desolation and rage when he returned, scared Violet.

"Where are you going?" Noah asked.

"To look for Snapper. If I can't find Jordan's killer, at least maybe I can find his dog."

"It's too late in the day, Zach," Noah said. "Sun's setting and you've been hard at it. Sit back down and eat your supper."

Zach's eyes flashed blue fire. "I'm off duty so I'll do what I please. Or are you giving me orders on how to spend my off-hours now, too?"

Without waiting for an answer, he stalked out.

Noah blew out a long, slow breath and closed his eyes for a moment.

Violet's stomach knotted watching him. She ached for what she understood must be his feeling of painful helplessness at days, weeks, of agony with no progress toward solving his brother's murder. Now added to that was another case that was seemingly stymieing the police. The burdens were almost too much to take for all of them.

"Do we just let him go?" Finn said. "Walk out when he's in that state of mind?"

Carter sighed. "Can't stop him. We have to hope and pray that he doesn't self-destruct or do something dumb."

Violet knew she had to act fast before her father tried to stop her. Quickly, she went to the kitchen and hung up her apron, grabbed her phone and slipped out the back door.

Hoping and praying were one thing, but she wasn't about to let Zach go off by himself.

SIXTEEN

Zach was just about to rocket out of the diner parking lot when Violet slid into the passenger seat next to him.

Eddie yipped in pleasure from the backseat.

Zach kept his gaze aimed stonily out the front windshield. “Not a good idea right now, Vi.”

“Why? Because you’re upset?”

“Because I’m not good company.”

“Well, you’re not tearing off alone, not like this.”

He gripped the steering wheel. “I’m too angry, Vi. I don’t want you to see me like this.”

“I’m big enough to take it.” She pointed a finger to the sky. “He is, too.”

"Don't talk to me about God. If you insist on coming along, at least spare me that, huh? People have been telling me all about God's love since I was a kid and right now, I just don't feel it."

"All right. We'll talk about whatever you want."

"I don't want to talk at all."

"That's fine, too. Drive on, Officer."

Muttering, he put the car in gear and drove, with no particular destination in mind. His thoughts whirled and churned inside. Jordy's killer was free to roam the streets and even kill again if he wanted to, and they had not one clue as to the person's motive or identity. Nothing. Hearing the coroner confirm what they already knew burned it deeper, like slowly dripping acid. They drove in silence until he found himself at Vanderbilt Parkway, where Jordy ran almost every day and had loved taking Ellie and Snapper to play on the weekends. Zach had no doubt Jordy would have continued the practice with his own son or daughter, if he hadn't been robbed of his chance to be a father. The place was quiet, the swing still, the slides empty. A man walked by with his dog, enjoying the evening air, and Zach's worry for Snapper flared anew.

Snapper was a gorgeous German shepherd, a highly trained officer, and Jordy had been proud of that dog, devoted to him. Zach and his brothers had spent hours scouring the place in case Snapper might have somehow returned. Was he even still alive? Try as he did to believe it, the likelihood was growing slimmer with each passing hour. As Zach watched the failing sunlight, his anger shifted to a sense of heavy despair that dragged down his soul.

Violet sat quietly next to him until the thoughts finally made their way out of his mouth.

"Snapper would never have allowed anything to happen to Jordy. The dog was protective, devoted, ferocious at times. I saw a drunk guy lurch at Jordy when we were working a Knicks game and Snapper went at him. Guy needed some serious first aid."

Violet sighed. "Beautiful dog."

"Yeah. Snapper would not have given up on Jordy unless..."

She reached over and squeezed his hand, knowing the rest.

Unless the murderer killed Snapper, too.

"I keep hoping that somehow Snapper got away," he said.

"I know. Me, too."

The weight became too much. "Why keep hoping, Vi? It's just going to hurt more when we find Snapper dead, if we ever find him at all." His voice broke. He gulped and tried again. "When I wake up in the morning, for a split second I forget what happened. I think that I'll find Jordy visiting in the first-floor kitchen, laughing and bragging about his dog and joking with Katie. And then I remember, and it's like I gotta grieve it all over again. It's like a punch in the gut, you know? Every single morning."

She nodded, face sculpted like marble in the dim light. So beautiful.

"I miss my brother." He felt hot tears on his face, but he didn't have the energy to try and hide them from her, so he closed his eyes and let them flow.

He felt her fingers capture his hand between her palms and she started to pray. At first, anger flashed inside him and he wanted to pull away from her, but again, he didn't have it in him to do anything but surrender to the pain. He allowed her words to cascade over him, through him, to tangle with the rage and grief and despair. They settled into the black pit where he'd landed the moment he understood his brother truly was gone, sending ripples through the mire. He did not know how long they stayed there, praying, but when he finally opened his eyes, the sun had fully faded to nighttime and the agony inside him had lessened a degree. The pain remained intense, but for some reason he no longer felt completely alone in bearing it.

He looked at her, at the tender smile she gave him. "I'm glad God gave me you," he choked out, pulling her hand to his mouth and kissing the knuckles.

"Ditto," she said, her own eyes glittering with tears.

"You still pray for me?"

"Every day, every hour, sometimes."

"Good, because I'm still wrecked inside, and I can't talk to God about it. There's just too much pain in between us. I'm so angry."

"He'll wait until you are ready. He's amazing that way."

His feelings became too much to hold inside. "You're amazing, Vi," he said, and he meant it. "All the issues you're dealing with right now, and you come along to help me."

Something hitched in her smile then. "You'd do it for me."

"I'd try." He reached out a hand to cup

her cheek and everything in him wanted to pull her close for another kiss. He pictured his cop brothers and sisters back in the diner, Violet's mom and dad, what they would say about him kissing her. And what if that kiss sent her running away, the truest friend he'd ever known? What if he drove this magnificent woman from his life? It would be the final loss, the blow that truly destroyed him. He ached to cross the inches between them, and feared what would happen if he did.

He let his arm trail away and scrubbed a hand over his face, clearing his throat. "I'll take you home."

Without waiting for an answer, he started to drive. The quiet in the car was mirrored in the scant traffic around them. New York was a city that truly never slept, but at that moment it was quieter, slower. They sat side by side in easy silence, something he shared with no other woman, no other person.

After a few blocks she sat back, cleared

her throat and smoothed her jeans. “I need to go by my apartment.”

“Why?”

“I could tell you, but you’re not going to like it.”

He heaved out a sigh and shifted in the driver’s seat. Though he’d made no breakthroughs and his troubles had not eased one tiny fraction, somehow his heart felt lighter after his time with Violet. “We’ll be stuck in traffic anyway, so you might as well spill it, Griffin.”

“All right,” she said, cocking her chin at him, “but don’t say I didn’t warn you.”

It was good to have details to discuss. Her nerves were still tumbling after her conversation with Zach. He’d delved deep into the private place where he locked all his feelings and brought some out to lay at her feet. It was a magnificent act of trust and she was honored beyond measure. She would have been happy to stay there and listen to him for hours, but she could tell by the weary slump to his shoulders that the storm had passed temporarily, and he needed to get some rest.

Don't worry, Zach. I will pray for you until you can see the daylight again.

"So why the urgent need to go back to your apartment?" he pressed.

She figured the best way was to flat-out say it. "I need to pick up a dress."

"A dress? No way. Beck might be watching. Buy yourself a new one."

"Are you volunteering to be my personal bodyguard while I go dress shopping? Just to let you know, that usually involves several stores and a minimum four hours or so."

He rolled his eyes. "That's nuts."

"Then you'll agree it's a better choice to let me pick up the dress I already have in my closet."

His brows crimped. "May I ask why you

need this garment? Sounds fancy for working in a diner and babysitting Latte."

She blew out a breath and steeled herself. "Bill Oscar's memorial ceremony is Monday."

He cut her off. "No."

"It's at a little room in the airport."

"No."

"And it will be well secured."

"No, Vi," he said, finally looking at her. "There is no way you should go to Bill's memorial service with Beck still at large."

"Come with me, then. If he makes a move, you'll be right there and you can arrest him."

"I'm not willing to risk your safety, and you shouldn't be, either. Let's be smart here."

"Zach, Bill was trying to save me." Her throat began to close and tears blurred her vision as much as she tried to keep them at bay. "He died, trying to warn me. He left behind a wife and two boys whom I have known since they were born. I have to be there for them."

Zach groaned. "Vi, you're killing me."

"I'm sorry. I don't want to make things harder, but I have to do this."

He gripped the wheel. "And I'm not going to change your mind no matter what I say?"

She shook her head.

He groaned. "At least you gave me some warning. I'll be with you every moment, of course."

Relieved, she settled back in the seat and let Zach drive back to her apartment. He looked so exhausted, eyes smudged with fatigue. Probably he was hungry, too, since he'd walked out in the middle of dinner. When they took the elevator up to her apartment, she pointed to the sofa. "You can sit on the end that isn't chewed and rest a while. It's going to take me a bit to try on the dress again. There's actually two choices, a black sheath, which is classic, but there's also…"

He waved a hand. "Right. Okay. Eddie

and I will just camp out on what's left of your sofa."

She went to the kitchen and returned with a bowl of cereal, a container of milk and a spoon. "Wheat squares. Dinner of champions, since you were silly enough to walk out on my father's clam chowder."

"Silly men get wheat squares, I guess. Thanks, Vi."

"You're welcome."

She went about her task of picking out a dress, finally settling on the black sheath and leather pumps, which she put into a duffel bag, along with more clothes and toiletries since she doubted she'd get Zach to agree to bring her back anytime soon.

A low rumble sounded from the living room. Eddie was asleep and snoring, curled up in Zach's lap. Zach was also asleep, head slanted to rest on her uncomfortable, half-eaten couch. They should go, get out of that apartment and back to the safety of the diner, but her heart swelled at the sight of him there, sleeping. His face was younger in sleep, not quite so careworn, and he almost looked like the high school boy she remembered, always with a basketball in his hand, looking for mischief and rarely still. She allowed herself a moment to take in the strong planes of his face, the angular chin, before she laid a quilt gently around his shoulders.

No reason why he can't have an hour of sleep before he takes me home.

Leaving him there asleep, she curled up in her favorite chair and tried to look at a fashion magazine. Her mind kept drifting back to the car, when she thought for a thunderous moment that he might kiss her again. The problem was, she desperately wanted him to, craved it with all her being.

The truth glided in, easy as a spring breeze. Oh, how she'd loved that man, craved moments with him, stored up their fond memories like a child collects shells on the beach. She'd broken her own rules with

Zach, revealed to him her soft fragile feelings and allowed him to become the most important person in her life.

Zach's lashes fluttered, and he sighed in his sleep. He was perfect for all his glaring imperfections, her heart's desire, right there on her lumpy sofa. She was fooling herself to claim anything else. She loved Zach Jameson, always had and probably always would. But that was where it had to stop, because he did not feel the same way and she could never risk losing him as a friend, her rock, her hero. If holding back her heart was the only way to preserve their friendship, then she would do it. The pain of it drove her to her feet and sent her pacing the confines of the living room.

She wandered to the window and looked down on the city street. It was dark now, but that did not completely stop the flow of New York City bustle. People traveled, even at this hour, along the sidewalks, and the parade of cars continued, along with the accompanying honking. She loved the city and it pained her as much as her father to see the little mom-and-pop shops and old brick storefronts giving way to gentrification. Why did progress have to mean losing the history and heartbeat of a community? In the glow from a streetlight, she saw a figure leaning, dark jacket, light T-shirt, the glowing tip of a cigarette poking through the gloom. It was impossible to see the face from such a distance, but the traffic headlights played over the bare head of the stranger long enough for her to catch his silhouette.

She sucked in a breath and stepped quickly out of view. Beck. He was watching the building, waiting for her and Zach to come out. Zach appeared at her elbow, rubbing his eyes. "What is it? Why did you let me sleep?"

"It's Beck, leaning against the lamppost."

Zach was instantly alert, grabbing his cell

phone. “I’ll get backup. Grab your stuff. We’ll take the stairs out the rear exit.”

Beck vanished from sight as Violet pulled back the curtain. She grabbed her bag and waited for Zach to make contact, half listening to the conversation over the rush of her own panicked breathing.

“Carter’s nearby, visiting a friend,” Zach said. “Local cops are responding, too.”

When he finally disconnected, she asked, “Won’t we be safer up here?”

Her question was answered for her when a face appeared at the fire escape and Beck’s boot smashed through the window.

Zach propelled her through the door and out into the hallway. “Go. Now.”

SEVENTEEN

They raced with Eddie past the elevator, which was making its way up to the third floor. Would the doors open to reveal another killer? If Violet wasn't with him, he'd take cover and wait to find out, but he couldn't risk a shoot-out, not with her close and the apartment walls so thin. Instead, he pushed her behind him as they ran to the stairwell. Clear. They scampered down two floors.

His heart was thundering the whole way. The patrol cops would be closing in on Beck as quick as they could, but traffic was impactful even for cars with sirens on the top.

One more floor and still no sign of Beck or anyone else. Heading onto the final descent, he nearly plowed into a middle-aged guy with headphones. Zach pulled his gun. The man blinked in shock and simultaneously dropped his water bottle.

"This is Mr. Gabriel," Violet said. "He walks up and down the stairs for exercise. Oh, we're terribly sorry, sir."

"Uh, no problem." Mr. Gabriel stepped aside. "People with guns and badges and dogs have the right of way."

"Did you see anyone else?" Zach said.

"No, but I didn't go outside. I just walk the stairs. It's dangerous out there."

Zach nodded grimly. He didn't know the half of it.

"This is my floor," Mr. Gabriel said.

"Get to your apartment and lock yourself in. Violet, take Eddie and go with him. If it's clear, I'll come back and get you."

Mr. Gabriel edged away. Violet hesitated. "And if it's not safe?"

"Tell Mr. Gabriel to call the cops."

"But you're the cops."

He laughed. “Carter will tell you I’m not as good as I think I am.”

“He’d be wrong.”

“Thanks for the vote of confidence.”

Violet stood against the wall as he went by. He pushed out into the night and crouched behind a stack of pallets while his vision adjusted. The traffic noise drifted from the street; the lot appeared empty. Nonetheless, he stayed there with his gun in his hand, listening, letting his eyes adjust to the dark. A noise pricked his ears. At first, he thought what he heard was the scuffling of claws from some rat or mouse. The sound grew more definite the longer he listened.

Then there was the tiny tapping noise, like fingers poking out a text message, from behind the hulk of a dumpster to his right. Steeling himself against the smell of rotting garbage, Zach crept around, easing into every step so he would not broadcast his presence.

When he was two feet away from the

edge of the dumpster, he raised his gun to firing position and readied himself.

Slow count of three, Zach.

Silently, he ticked off the time, but as he made his move, a twig snapped under his feet. A figure took off with a cry, sprinting away from the dumpster. Zach holstered his weapon and gave chase. If he hadn't been in prime basketball shape, Zach would have lost him. As it was he barely kept pace, shouting, "Stop, police!" to no avail. They were rapidly closing in on a chain-link fence that separated the lot from the main street. The guy, clearly not Beck, didn't slow and neither did Zach. He hurtled up the chain link like a cat, Zach right behind him, grabbing a handful of the guy's sweatshirt and pulling him down to the ground. They rolled over the damp asphalt, the man wriggling, eel-like, and Zach doing his best to wrench his arms behind his back. He'd almost succeeded in doing so when a vicious bark made them both jerk.

Carter appeared at a run, holding a straining Frosty, who was yanking and tugging at the leash. Maddeningly, Violet stood a few feet away with Eddie.

"Get back, Vi. He could have a gun," Zach shouted.

"Stop resisting or I'm going to send in the dog," Carter yelled.

"No," the man said, going suddenly still. "I'm unarmed. Don't let the dog get at me. Please."

Zach kept his full body weight on the guy. "I'm going to cuff your hands. If you try to get away, you're gonna get shot or bitten. Got me?"

He nodded, eyes fastened on Frosty. Canine officers had that effect on certain suspects. Noting Frosty's laser-beam focus, Zach could understand the feeling.

Meeting no further resistance, Zach rolled the man on his stomach and cuffed his wrists behind his back. "You can sit up. Slowly. Don't do anything dumb."

The man complied and Zach got a good look at him. “You work at the furniture store. You were trying to keep me from buying a table. Name?”

“Hugo Clark.”

Zach found Hugo’s phone on the ground, the last text he’d been ready to send still on the screen.

In position in back.

“Who told you to watch the building?”

Hugo grimaced. “I was helping a friend.”

“Who?”

Hugo didn’t answer.

“A guy named Beck?”

No answer.

“You know you’re going to jail?”

“What for? I didn’t do anything.”

“I’m going to trace the number you’ve been texting and find out it belongs to Xavier Beck, a wanted murderer.” It was conjecture, unlikely to happen. The phones were probably all disposable, untraceable. "You're an accomplice."

"I didn't know what he was going to do. I had to help him."

"Why?"

Hugo looked at his shoes. "Same reason I follow orders at the furniture store."

"Who's your boss?"

Again no answer.

Zach took a risk. It had to be connected to the mastermind running drugs through the airport and furniture store. "Is it Uno?"

Clark's mouth dropped open, but he quickly recovered. "I don't know who you're talking about."

"I'm talking about the guy who's running a smuggling operation here in Queens. Where can I find him?"

No answer.

"You tell me, or you go to jail."

Hugo threw his head back. "I choose jail."

"So be it. Stay still and don't move or you're the dog's chew toy." When another officer arrived, Hugo was bundled off. Zach walked a few paces away to confer with Carter and Violet.

He glared at Violet. "And I'm sure you have a good reason for putting yourself at risk by coming out here?"

She looked chagrined. "I was watching out Mr. Gabriel's window. I saw Carter and I sort of followed."

He could not trust himself to reply to her so he faced Carter. "Took you a while to get here," Zach grumped.

Carter shrugged. "Traffic." He lowered his voice. "We didn't get Beck, by the way. Patrol cop said he bailed when he spotted us as your backup."

Zach groaned. "And we've got another guy who's so scared about this Uno that he will choose jail over ratting his boss out."

"Might be a good way to stay alive, plus Victor Jones was bailed out within twenty-four hours, so Hugo's probably figuring his loyalty will be rewarded."

"And he's no doubt correct," Violet said. "But it's all right. Beck didn't get to me and you weren't hurt."

He wiped the sweat from his brow and took the leash from Violet.

No, he wanted to tell her. *It's not anywhere close to being all right.*

He shot a look at Frosty, who was still staring fixedly at Hugo. "If you had released him, he would have known I was the good guy, right?"

Carter gave a nonchalant shrug and grinned. "Probably."

Zach did not say the thoughts that scrolled across his mind.

When they drove back to the diner at Violet's insistence late that evening, the team met him there, their collective brows creased in worry. He reported every detail that might be remotely helpful in catching Beck, but once again the guy had vanished.

"We've got to catch a break here sometime," Brianne said.

A smile broke over Finn Gallagher as he looked at his phone, excitement projected on his genial face. He stood up, straightening his broad shoulders. "I think we just did, but it's about another case. I have some news."

"Please let it be good this time," Brianne said. "I'm sick of the bad kind."

"Oh, yeah. I think this qualifies. Check out the picture that was sent to our tip line." Finn was a perpetual jokester, but this time Zach knew he wasn't kidding around.

They all crowded around to see Finn's screen.

Zach's nerves jumped as he peered at the grainy photo. "That's..."

"Snapper," Finn finished. "In all his big, bad, canine glory."

The image was slightly blurred, a large German shepherd caught from the side, powerful, mottled black and silver. The animal was all coiled energy, as if he was just about to sprint out of the camera view. Jordan's police dog. It had to be.

Zach pumped his fist, overflowing with sudden optimism. "Yes, he's survived somehow." The elation was almost too much to contain. "Where was the picture taken?"

"Queensbridge Park," Finn said. "We've got people there now, but I assume you'll all want to head over there on your off time and look."

"You assumed right," Carter said.

Gavin cleared his throat. "I feel like I should advise us to exercise caution here." He folded his long arms, brown eyes serious, though his tone was gentle. Zach had always appreciated Gavin's thoughtful demeanor, but at that moment it rubbed him the wrong way.

"What?" Finn said. "Why?"

"It might not be what we want it to be," Gavin said. "That's all."

Zach rounded on him. "You have something to say?"

"I don't want everyone getting their hopes up. We don't have anything definitive. There are lots of German shepherds in New York. That dog might not be Snapper."

"There's a harness in the photo..." Brianne started.

"Only part of it is visible, no NYPD markings. The photo is blurry. I'm being practical."

"You're being obstinate because you're still angry," Zach snapped.

Gavin's mouth tightened. "Wouldn't you be? If your brothers in blue accused you of murdering the chief?"

"No one accused you," Noah said.

"Might as well. You were all ready to pin me for it."

"There was bad blood between you and Jordy. He got the job you felt you were entitled to."

"The job I felt I'd earned," Gavin said. "There's a long way from professional competition to murder. I thought you all knew me better than that."

"It's over," Noah said. "We have to get past it if we're going to function as a unit and close the case."

"Easy for you to say." Gavin's expression was bitter. "You're the chief and a Jameson. You're not on the outside looking in."

"Hey," Zach said, his voice rising above the collected murmurs. "What's important here and now is my brother's dog. I am choosing to believe that Snapper's alive until I'm proven wrong."

"Me, too," Carter said.

Noah, Brianne and Finn added their approval.

"Believe it or not," Gavin said, "that's what I want to think, too. We should tread cautiously is all I'm saying."

"Fair enough," Noah said. "Cautiously."

Zach didn't say anything. He intended to search long and hard until Snapper was brought home and if that meant taking risks, so be it.

If you're alive, Snapper, we'll find you. I promise.

Violet was thrilled to listen in on Finn's good news from the kitchen as she busied herself with closing-up chores. She'd insisted on returning to the diner because there was no safer place. The comfort of pots and pans, the hum of conversation, the armor of an apron wrapped around her—somehow these things would protect her from the fear that robbed her of her self-confidence, one violent confrontation after another.

The long moments in the stairwell before Carter had arrived permeated her consciousness as she'd worried for her own safety and Zach's. Beck could have been waiting in ambush. Would she ever again live a life without fear?

Zach followed her into the kitchen.

"That's wonderful news about Snapper. When will you go out and search?"

"Brianne and Finn are going now. I'll join them once I know you're tucked in for the night."

She waited for the inevitable and it didn't take long for him to get around to the topic.

"Of course, the memorial is out of the question now."

"I'm busy, Zach. Look at this sink full of dishes. Gotta have this place in order for the breakfast service." She plunged her hands into the soapy water, surprised when he did the same, mechanically scrubbing the dishes and handing them to her for rinsing. They were up to the third dish before he started to hammer his point home again.

"After tonight you can see that Beck's got help, the furniture store people, plenty of eyes on you everywhere."

The fear balled together inside her, forming something rigid and angry. She squirted in more dish soap and slammed on the hot water. "Zach, I am going to the memorial."

"No, you're not."

"Yes, I am, and your bossiness isn't going to change that."

He clutched a soapy dish, water streaming everywhere. "Vi, knock it off."

"You're the one who should knock it off and stop dripping water all over the floor."

He lowered it quickly, smacking it on the side of the sink and chipping off a piece.

"Now, see? You broke another dish." She turned off the water with a jerk.

"With good reason. You're making me crazy." He was talking loudly now so she raised her voice over him.

"I wouldn't be forced to stand my ground if you weren't bullying me."

"I am not bullying you. I'm just trying to get you to understand..." Zach started.

The door to the kitchen swung open and her father stuck his head in. "You two are bickering so loud we can hear it the next room. We're all trying to plan out the Snapper search times. Can you keep it down to a dull roar?"

Zach blew out a breath. "Sorry, Lou."

He shook his head. "No wonder Jordy used to say you sounded like an old married couple." He took in Violet's steely glare and raised a bushy eyebrow at Zach. "You need some backup in here, son?"

"No, sir. I can handle it."

Her father smiled. "Oh, I doubt that, but I admire your pluck." Chuckling, he withdrew.

Zach waited until the door closed again. Jaw clenched, he spoke in a hard, controlled tone.

"You cannot go to that memorial, Vi. It's dangerous."

"I know that."

"Then make an excuse."

She began to stack the wet, clean dishes, one at a time, punctuating with each dish.

"I will not... I can not...allow these creeps to take away my life."

"They aren't..."

The tension of the past hours, their frantic flight down her apartment stairs, began to bubble up inside her. "They are," she spat. "I have had to leave my job, my apartment, and I've had to watch you risk your safety for mine." Tears threatened but she would not let them fall. "I won't let them take away my final goodbye to Bill."

"It's not worth it."

"It's worth it to me."

"You're scared. It's bringing out your stubborn side."

"Yes, I'm scared." She saw her own emotion mirrored in the blue of his eyes. She saw what he must see: a small, frightened woman, powerless, losing her world one piece at a time. It made her stand up straighter, shoulders back. "I'm scared, but I'm not a coward. I will not give up what I've worked for, what I've earned."

He blew out a breath. “I’m not asking you to give it up, just put it on the shelf for a while.” The water splashes made dark patches on his shirt. “For me, Vi. Would you do it for me?”

“Zach, don’t you dare.” She put down the last dish so hard it cracked in two.

“Don’t start breaking dishes now, too, or they’ll come back and accuse us of being an old married couple again.”

He was trying to jolly her, but she was too far submerged in her roiling emotions. “I’m never going to marry.”

“That’s not true, of course you will.”

“No, I won’t.” Despair clattered through her along with the worry, frustration, anger at him, anger at herself and everything that had transpired since that fateful shift at the airport.

“Why not?”

Her filter failed completely, and she answered him with the truth. “Because I’ll never find anyone else like you.”

He stopped, stared, a dripping dish sprinkling moisture onto his steel-toed boots. "What did you say?"

Had she said it aloud? She desperately wanted to take it back, sponge the admission away, pretend she hadn't said it, make it into a joke, but his thunderstruck expression made it clear that the damage was irreversible. She might as well have admitted aloud she was in love with Zach Jameson. A wave of nausea almost made her wretch. What had she done? She could only stand there, mute.

He blinked several times and finally looked at the plate in his hand as if it had just appeared there. Slowly and carefully he put it down. "Uh, Vi, well, I mean, I didn't really..."

She snatched up a dish towel. "Never mind. I don't know why I said that. Forget it, okay?"

"It's fine and you know, sweet, but I figured, uh, I mean, we're friends, right?"

She nodded, willing him to stop talking.

"And, uh, that will never change."

Oh, but it had. In one careless moment she'd made him see her as a love-struck teen instead of a woman, a pining lover instead of his best friend. She could not speak.

He gave her a faltering smile. "No worries. It's okay. And we can discuss the memorial thing tomorrow. I've got to talk to Noah and then I'll escort you home."

"No," she said somehow. "I want to stay. Dad will take me home later after we close."

"Okay, but I'll wait around and follow you, just to be sure." He swiped at his shirt. "So, anyway, sorry I broke the dish."

"Don't worry about it." How she'd made her mouth say the words was a mystery.

I'll never find anyone else like you.

With seven little words, she'd just ruined everything. Mercifully, she was able to contain the tears until the doors swung shut behind him.

EIGHTEEN

Monday morning Zach tapped his spoon against his cereal bowl until his brother startled him from his reverie.

"What's got you all twisted up in knots?"

Zach looked up from his uneaten cereal at Carter. "Huh?"

Carter snapped his fingers as if to rouse Zach. "You're in la-la land. You've been staring at your cereal so long it's mush. Worried about the memorial today?"

"Yeah." He was, but something else was grabbing for his attention, too—the comment from Violet that beat like a drum in his memory.

I'll never find anyone else like you.

He couldn't quite wrap his mind around

Violet's bombshell from Saturday night. His tough girl had thoughts about him that were not merely friendly. The admission startled and confused him, especially when he added it together with his persistent desire to kiss her and the word *love* that continually cropped up in his mind at the drop of a hat. At Archie's apartment, he'd acted on impulse and she'd been merely surprised, not eager—hadn't she? Maybe he'd gotten it wrong. It wouldn't be the first time he'd misunderstood a woman. They were harder to read than the fine print on a medicine bottle. What if her feelings were growing as intense as his were?

"Carter, what does it mean when a woman says she'll never find anyone else like you?"

He screwed up his face in thought. "In your case, it could mean you're such a class-A dunce, she'll be hard-pressed to find anyone as clueless as you are."

"Thanks."

He slid into the chair opposite Zach. “Seriously though, who’s the woman?”

Zach shrugged. “Not important.”

“Uh-huh.” He folded his arms and perused Zach across the table.

Zach put the spoon down. “Go ahead and say whatever it is that’s on your mind. You’re dying to, anyway. I can tell, so we might as well get this over with.”

Carter lost the sarcastic edge. “I was just thinking that if you’ve got someone pining for you, it’s best to go slow, huh? Our lives are completely sideways right now, and you may not be firing on all cylinders in the love department.”

“Thanks for the vote of confidence.”

Carter frowned. “No dig intended. We’re all under a lot of stress. We may not be interpreting things exactly as we should be. I don’t want you to get hurt. Not sure you could take any more of that right now. Not sure any of us could.”

Zach should have been annoyed at his

brother's advice, but he found he was not. Perhaps he had misconstrued Violet's utterance, with all the upheaval in his own heart and mind. More than likely, he'd heard something that wasn't there. He felt calmer, and inexplicably sad. "I hear you. Thanks."

"Anytime. Ready for today?"

They'd gone over the security details plenty of times. Zach would be in uniform with Eddie, a deterrent to anyone looking to hurt Violet in the event housed in a small room at LaGuardia. Carter, Noah and Gavin would be fanned out in the parking lot to provide eyes on the attendees to Bill's memorial along with patrol officers. The rest of the department knew about the plans, as well. Since they would be stationed at the airport, they could be there at a moment's notice if necessary. He'd not been able to get Violet to agree to wear body armor. She hadn't even replied, just given him a look that said, "You are out of your mind." She was probably right.

He passed the time before he was to pick up Violet for the eleven o'clock event by working out and doing some training exercises with Eddie in the backyard. Eddie was obliging as usual, and Zach was pleased to see he'd not dug any more holes in the yard. He was grateful that he'd not transferred any of his emotional upheaval to his dog. They sat in the buttery sunshine for a few moments and he stroked the dog's silky ears. Eddie whined with delight and offered his tummy.

As he often did, Zach contemplated the people who had abandoned Eddie as a puppy. "Wonder who you lost, huh, buddy? Did you love the people who let you down in such a big way?"

Would Jordy be let down at the way his brother had handled his death? No, Jordy loved Zach, Carter, Noah and the whole K-9 unit, and Zach knew his feelings would not have changed in spite of their inability to thwart the murder or catch the perpetrator. Jordy would have understood, and he would have had wise counsel about Zach's current maelstrom of confusion about Violet. He was not sure exactly what advice his brother would have given, but he knew it would have ended with, "Why don't you pray about it?"

Prayer. Zach didn't know how anymore. There was too much anger at God, too much sorrow, and he did not even know what to ask about his feelings for Violet. Nevertheless, the urge to pray pressed down through his reticence and he closed his eyes.

"Lord… I don't understand You and I don't think I even like You right now, but…" He swallowed. "I'll trust You. You promised peace and rest and safety, so I'm asking You to make good on that promise. Not for me, but for Vi. I'm not enough for her, or anybody else, but the Bible says You are, so I'll try to hang on to that."

When he opened his eyes, there was no change, no insight that might order his unsettled feelings, but he felt inexplicably better, lighter, somehow.

He caressed the dog sprawled across his legs. "So all we have to do is keep Violet safe, bring down Xavier Beck and whomever he's working for, find Jordy's killer and locate Snapper if he's still alive. Think we can do all that, Ed?"

The dog wagged his tail with effervescent canine optimism and beamed his soulful brown eyes at Zach.

"That's what I thought you'd say. Let's do this, Officer Eddie."

Eddie flapped his ears and followed Zach to the car.

Violet was as carefully put together as she could possibly be. Her hair was gathered into soft waves at the back of her neck thanks to several clips and a deep conditioning treatment. The black sheath was perfectly fitted, with a light sweater to cover her bare shoulders. For a touch of color, she'd gone with the silk scarf that her father had given her on her sixteenth birthday.

Because a woman should have something nice from her daddy, he'd said. The memory made her smile. Her father was probably pacing the floor at the diner right now, regardless of all her reassurance that nothing could possibly go wrong with so many safety plans in action.

"There were plenty of security people at the airport during your shift, too, and that's where all this trouble started in the first place," he'd replied.

She slipped on her black heels as Zach knocked.

"Zach and Eddie's taxi service," he called through the door. "Here for a pickup, ma'am."

Smiling, she opened it, gratified when his mouth fell open.

"Man, you look amazing."

Warmth tickled her cheeks at his flat-out

admiration. "Thank you. Too bad it's for such a sad occasion."

He cocked his head. "You look perfect, Vi, except for one tiny thing. You know what would complete the outfit?"

She held up a finger. "If you say a bullet-proof vest, I'm going to call for a real taxi."

He closed his mouth and sighed. "All right. It was worth a try. After you."

The private reception was held at LaGuardia, in a small room that backed the tarmac. It was an event solely for those employees who had worked with Bill. Another family ceremony would take place the following week. The roar of airplane traffic had to be dampened by extra insulation and heavy draperies on the walls. She knew, because she'd been there before, when they'd lost another coworker to a heart attack and Bill had arranged a lovely ceremony complete with a buffet luncheon. The memory made her tear up, but she tried some deep breathing. It would not help Bill's wife to have Violet fall apart at the event. She'd spoken to Rory several times on the phone, arranged for a meal to be delivered and agonized that she could not bring it personally, helped create a guest list from the airline employees who would be eager to attend the memorial.

If Beck wasn't caught, she realized, then Rory would be affected, too, perhaps never seeing justice served for her husband, her boys growing up with the knowledge that no one had been punished for taking away their father. Beck's violence had robbed them all of so much. She felt Zach's palm on the small of her back as they approached the room.

"You don't have to do this."

"Yes, I do," she said, but she was not sorry that he kept his hand there as they walked inside. The room was set up with a large photo of Bill staged on an easel. The picture captured his humble demeanor, the friendly smile. The sight of it made her breath catch.

Rory looked tired and wan, but she greeted Violet with an embrace.

"The boys are at home with their grandma. They could hardly stand me leaving them today." She caught her lip between her teeth. "Actually, I'm not sure I can take it, either. I didn't sleep at all last night."

"I'm so sorry," Violet said.

Rory looked past Violet at Zach and her mouth tightened. "My husband wasn't a criminal. He just got caught up with the wrong people."

Zach tipped his head. "My condolences, ma'am. I am sorry for your loss."

She glared at him, gaze sweeping the floor. "I don't want a dog in here."

"I apologize, ma'am. I know this is a terrible time for you. Eddie will not disrupt the proceedings in any way, I promise."

"Well, at least keep him away from the food, will you?"

"Yes, ma'am."

She whirled on her heel.

"You can understand how she feels," Violet said.

"I do. I'll try to stay as unobtrusive as possible."

Not easy for a six-foot uniformed cop with a beagle sitting at his feet. Violet left him, to greet her fellow airline workers, many of whom were holding back tears. When the proceedings started, Violet listened to her colleagues talk about Bill and she tried not to let loose with her own tears. How could he be gone, yanked so abruptly away from all these people who loved him? Zach stood in the back, Eddie's nose twitching at the swirl of odors all around him.

The smell of the food, sandwiches, cheese platters and crudités set out on a skirted table, made her stomach churn. The room grew warm and she turned to slip off her sweater. She looked out the sliver of a window. Her heart stopped as she saw Beck. He pointed directly at her.

"Gotcha," he mouthed, and he smiled.

NINETEEN

Zach saw Violet's face slacken with horror. He followed her line of sight in time to see a quick glimpse of Beck's profile before he disappeared from the window. Immediately, Zach walked to Violet.

"Come with me. Now."

People looked at them, startled, but he took Violet's arm and urged her to the opposite exit, which led to the area where his car was parked. He radioed Carter, stationed at the rear, and informed him about Beck.

"I don't see him. There's something going down on the tarmac. Gavin, you copy?"

"Ten-four. Tower reports a fire on one of the runways. Sending personnel."

Zach's nerves flooded with adrenaline. "It's gotta be a diversion."

The air erupted with the wail of distant sirens as the firefighters raced to respond.

Then there was the sound of gunfire. Energy roared through Zach in a tidal wave. Though everything in him wanted to run and back up his brother and Gavin, he knew what he had to do. He burst out into the hallway, hurrying Violet, Eddie following along. They'd exited through the side, staying as far away from Beck as possible.

The radio chatter proved that Noah was rolling to assist Carter and Gavin, bringing in more reinforcements as the runways were shut down. Zach was four feet past the exit doors when a baggage truck careened up to them, pulling a canvas-sided cart behind it, Beck at the wheel. Zach froze. Beck must have used his inside man, Jeb Leak, gotten access and set the whole diversion in motion.

Zach turned and reached for his weapon

when a sharp blow to the skull sent him to the ground. His radio was yanked from his grasp, his gun stripped from his holster. Sparks exploded in his skull but he forced his eyes open to see a gun pressed to Violet's temple by Xavier Beck. Eddie barked wildly, his leash tucked into the fist of Victor Jones, the one who'd hit him.

"Stupid dog. Quit your yapping." Victor rolled Zach onto his stomach, looping a length of duct tape around his wrists. Zach fought, twisting his head to keep his sights on Violet, but Jones had the leverage and he felt the weight of a boot crushing into his spine.

Beck loomed above him. "Well, if it isn't Officer Do Right. It's time to go on a little trip." Zach tried to roll over, but instead Jones yanked him by his bound wrists to his feet. Unzipping the canvas siding on the cart, he propelled him inside. The truck concealed their actions, the airport vehicle a perfect way to blend into the chaos.

"What should we do with the dog?" Jones said.

Beck snorted. "Shoot it. I hate dogs."

"No," Zach said, thrashing and kicking.

"Don't kill the dog," Violet said. He could hear her panicky breathing, but her voice was the calm tone honed from years of airline service. "If you shoot now, they'll hear. You'll have cops all over you."

The seconds ticked by with Zach shouting and kicking, until Beck came into view, the gun pressed so hard to Violet's head that he could see a red mark forming.

"If you continue to struggle, I will hurt her. You get me?"

Zach stopped, chest heaving, rage roaring like an inferno inside him. "If you hurt her, it will be the last thing you ever do."

Beck laughed. "Big words, Do Right," he said. "Move over and make room for your lady friend and the mutt."

Jones forced Violet into the cart next to him and Eddie was tossed on Violet's lap.

She cradled the dog with trembling hands and worked to soothe him. Eddie whined and tried to get to Zach, but she held him.

Beck got behind the wheel. Victor climbed into the cart and partially zipped the canvas. Then he turned sideways with a gun aimed at them. "Make trouble and I start shooting," he said. "It will get really messy, really fast."

Zach stared him down. "Where are you taking us? You'll never get off the runway. Cops are everywhere. You got a flying carpet or something?"

Eyeing him in the rearview mirror, Jones answered. "You guessed, Do Right. I didn't think you had the smarts." He pointed to the end of the farthest runway. "Got ourselves a private cargo plane. No frills, but very roomy. We're leaving the country for a while until things cool down. We needed a little insurance policy to get away, what with all the cop activity you've brought down on us."

Leaving the country. A death sentence for both of them, or worse. “Take me, then,” Zach said. “A cop for a hostage, not her. Let her go.”

“Oh, we will take you. And when we get close to our destination, we’ll toss you out, but she’s coming, too. Nice to have someone around who can cook and clean.”

Violet glared at him. “In your dreams.”

He laughed. “Kidding. You’re a witness, after all, so Beck says it will be a one-way trip for you, too.”

Zach yanked at the duct tape that bound his wrists behind him. His brothers had to have seen Beck’s vehicle speeding away. Were they right behind him?

“The airport is locked down. You won’t make it out of here.”

“No problem,” Jones said. “We’ll be aboard and in the air in minutes.”

In the air, cut off from any help. He could not let that happen.

As they sped toward a looming cargo

plane, Zach nudged Violet with his knee. She jerked a look at him and he tried to wriggle his hands while Jones studied the tarmac through the partially unzipped canvas. She understood. Since Eddie created some concealment, she snaked one arm behind Zach. With her manicured fingernails, she scratched and probed until she found the edge of the duct tape. The truck was moving fast now, the cart bumping and shimmying. Violet kept focused, prying the tape up with agonizing slowness, but she had to stop every time Jones shot a glance at them.

In the distance, he heard sirens and hope surged inside him. His brothers were on their way with plenty of units. He just needed to get free and keep Violet safe until backup arrived. The cargo plane came into view. He could not figure out how Beck had gotten weapons past security and onto the runway.

He felt the tape loosen slightly and he

could barely keep still. Eddie whined as a bump jarred him from Violet's lap and sent him falling off. Violet stopped pulling at the tape and helped Eddie scramble into her protection again. Another few tugs and the tape loosened more, but she had to stop again as Beck braked to a standstill.

Beck came around and pulled Violet from the car while Jones did the same to Zach. He tied Eddie to the empty baggage cart. Eddie's shrill baying was lost in the shriek of sirens. Jones shoved them both up the ramp and onto the plane. With a brutal push, he knocked them to their knees on the floor. All around them were stacks of furniture, tied down and secure, and all no doubt filled with hidden drugs.

Zach frantically worked at the duct tape, praying that Violet had weakened the bonds. The tape began to stretch, buying him precious inches to work his wrists back and forth. He ignored the pain and the warmth of the blood caused by the abrasion. A minute more was all he needed.

"Cops have figured out our diversion. They're blocking the runway," Jones shouted.

"Take them down," Beck snapped. Jones started shooting. Bullets pounded toward the blockade of police cars, toward his brothers. Every muscle in Zach's body was wire taut. Noah's voice came out tinny and distorted over his public address channel.

"Xavier Beck, this is the NYPD. You are completely surrounded and there's no way out. Hijack protocols are in place and this airport is locked down. Release your hostages immediately and order your pilot to cut the engines."

Beck answered by firing his own weapon, too. Noah's words were lost in the barrage of bullets.

"We're taking off now," Beck yelled to the pilot through the open cockpit door.

"Air traffic control has ordered me to turn

off the engines," the pilot answered, peeking out, sweat beading his forehead. "This isn't worth what you're paying me. This wasn't what I signed on for."

"If you power down," Beck snarled, "I will shoot you right now and fly this plane myself."

The pilot's lips moved but he did not speak. "Mr. Beck, there is no way…even if we get in the air…"

Beck cut him off. "I have a boss to answer to who won't settle for your death as a punishment. He'll make sure everyone you ever loved dies, too, slowly and painfully. You get me?"

Gulping, the pilot nodded and turned back to the controls.

The plane rumbled as the pilot began to ready for takeoff. Jones braced himself against the wall and kept his gun trained on them while Beck supervised the pilot. Zach yanked at the duct tape, desperate now.

If they got off the ground, they would

not survive. Violet turned a terrified gaze at him, the brown of her eyes clouded in disbelief. She trusted him to keep her safe, believed in him when he did not believe in himself. And he realized in that moment that his heart would not continue to beat if hers didn't, that the cascade of confusing feelings he'd felt toward her had crystallized into one clear and shining reality: he loved her, adored her, and he was about to lose her.

The seconds ticked away as the plane began to roll down the runway.

Violet's body shook from the vibrations of the plane and her own bone-deep fear. They were trapped in a nightmare. Beck was crazy to send the plane right into the police barricade and ignore what would have to be a massive response from Homeland Security to an airport breach. Hijacking protocols in the post 9-11 days were clear. Even if the plane somehow took off, it would be tracked until it landed and met with another mountain of security personnel. Beck was insane to think they would survive.

"Victor, listen," she started. "Beck is crazy. He'll get us all killed. You'll never..."

"Close the hatch," Beck shouted from the cockpit.

Jones jerked the gun at her. "You do it. Now."

She was crouched against a crate, trying to keep her balance as the plane lurched over the tarmac. Zach faced her, on his knees. He gave her a wink. What did it mean? She thought about their childhood when such a look meant, "Keep my secret, Vi. I'm going to launch a surprise attack on my brothers."

A surprise attack? No, her mind screamed. Jones could not miss at such a distance. Zach would be killed for sure. Then she saw Zach's arm come loose from behind him and there was no more time to stall.

She reached up as if to secure the hatch, but she pretended to stumble and fall with a dramatic scream thrown in for good measure.

As she'd hoped, Jones yanked a startled look at her just as Zach surged forward, a perfect football tackle that drove the air out of Jones's stomach.

He hurtled back, smashing into a metal edge, stunning himself. Violet grabbed up a flashlight secured to the wall and swung it at Jones's chin. The contact sent him toppling. His gun skittered across the floor and behind a table shrouded in blankets. He groaned and went still.

"Here," Zach said, gesturing with his bound hands.

She quickly unfastened the tape.

"Find the gun," Zach said, ripping the rest of the tape from his wrists. She darted toward the stacked furniture. The space was dark and she could not see the gun anywhere. Dropping to hands and knees, she felt along the grimy floor, fingers cold and shaking. Despair licked at her until she saw a corner of the weapon poking out from underneath a plastic-wrapped pallet.

"Got it," she said, but as she reached for it, a roar of rage stopped her.

"Get up," Beck boomed, emerging from the cockpit with murder in his eyes.

Their time had run out.

TWENTY

"It's all falling apart, Beck," Zach said, struggling to his feet. "You can't get away. It's over."

Noah's radio command cut through the din again. "Stop the plane, Beck. There's no way out."

"He's right. You're outgunned and outnumbered."

"I'll have help when we land this bucket. All I need to do is buy some time." He aimed the gun at Zach. "I think your body bouncing across the tarmac would do the trick."

"No!" Violet yelled. He pulled the trigger. Her scream mingled with the report of the gun.

He fired just as the plane juddered, upsetting his aim. The shot zinged into the ceiling, raining sparks down on Zach. Violet darted at Beck, grabbing at his arm but he jabbed an elbow into her ribs, driving the breath from her lungs and sending her falling to the floor.

"Get out, Violet!" Zach yelled. "Jump out now."

Instead, she tried to scramble to her feet, but the impact had made her dizzy. She tried again, upright just as Beck took aim at Zach and fired a round.

Again, the bullet went wide, but Zach stumbled to one knee. Beck took aim one last time and smiled. "Trip's over."

"No!" she screamed.

There was a flash of brown and for a moment she did not realize what was happening. Eddie leaped into the plane, trailing his chewed leash. He barked with everything in him, lunging for the man who was about to murder his master.

At the same time, Zach dived for Beck's gun hand while Eddie latched on to Beck's pant leg. The combination took Beck over backward. Zach and Beck rolled on the floor, grappling for control of the gun. Another shot let loose, ricocheting off the metal door frame in a shower of sparks.

"Violet, jump off!" Zach shouted again through gritted teeth. The muscles of his neck were banded steel as he fought Beck. "Now!"

An idea sparked. She ignored the command and whipped off her scarf, pulling it around Beck's neck.

With a strength she didn't know she possessed, she held it as tight as she could until Beck began to make gagging noises. Zach hammered away at Beck's fist until the gun popped loose.

Violet continued to hold as tight as her trembling muscles would allow until Beck went unconscious. Zach rolled him onto his stomach. "Tie his hands."

She did, making a mess of the knot, but securing him nonetheless. He was breathing, body limp. Zach grabbed Beck's gun and charged into the cockpit.

"Police! Stop this plane right now," Zach commanded.

"I will, I will. Just don't shoot," came the reply.

Violet felt the plane slow until it rolled to a stop. Zach led the pilot out into the cargo area. "On your belly on the floor. Don't move." He meekly followed instructions. Zach kept the gun trained on the two.

"Violet," he said over his shoulder. "There's gonna be an army of highly amped officers swarming this plane in a matter of moments. We're going to stay really still until they can secure the scene and show them we've got everything under control in here. Okay?"

"Okay," she whispered.

Eddie snuggled up to Zach's leg, whining and pawing.

"You did great, buddy," Zach said. "And you're completely forgiven for the sofa incident." Eddie whined. Zach glanced at Violet.

"You okay, Vi?"

She nodded.

His smile was nothing short of brilliant, despite the blood smeared on his brow and grime streaking his temple. "I knew you had it in you, Vi. Never doubted my tough girl for a moment."

"New York tough," she said, and then she started to cry.

As he figured, his fellow officers had arrived with guns drawn and ready for battle. They'd arrested the pilot, and taken Victor Jones and Xavier Beck via armed guard to the hospital before their inevitable arrest. Zach figured with ten cops watching their slightest twitch, there was no way they would escape custody. Roach was still at large, but he was a small-time player to this point, and not a threat to Violet. Zach was confident they'd get him in time, too. He was tired, bruised and bloody, but buzzing with sweet satisfaction. The three of them—a cop, an airline employee and a beagle—had taken down the bad guys and kept the plane on the ground. He'd even gotten word that Jeb Leak, the crooked TSA agent, had been taken into custody. He reveled in the victory, wishing Jordy were there to share it.

Noah broke away from his duties along with Carter to out-and-out force Zach over to the paramedic unit where Violet was being checked.

"I don't need..." he started.

"I don't care what you need," Noah said. "I want you to get checked out and I'm driving the chief's car last I checked, so get your scrawny carcass over there pronto."

Carter quirked a smile. "I'd follow orders if I were you."

"Yes, sir," he said.

"When you get the all clear for you and Violet, we'll meet back at Griffin's. I've already called Lou and Barbara to tell them it's over." Noah left to talk to the airport officials.

Zach shot a look at Violet, hunched over, wrapped in a blanket and talking quietly to the medics. "You know," he said, "she would have made a great cop if she'd wanted to."

Carter considered. "That right?"

"I mean, you should have been there. She was terrified, but she came through, anyway. Went after a guy with a gun using her scarf. I've been around cops all my life and I've never seen courage like that."

Carter raised an eyebrow. "She'd probably say you're pretty good in a crisis situation, too." He paused. "Might even say she'd never find someone else like you, huh?"

Zach jerked a look at him, warmth infusing his cheeks. "I… I feel… I mean I finally realized…" He simply could not get the words out that he was in love with Violet.

His brother laughed. “I get it. I think maybe you’d be a class-A dunce not to feel that way. Go do your thing, Zach.” Chuckling, Carter walked away.

Zach watched Violet for a moment. Something the medic said made her smile. That smile was worth everything they’d been through; it was priceless, breathtaking, one of a kind. The lights of the runway, the bustle of the police personnel and the sounds of the commotion all faded away as he looked at Violet, his best friend, and so much more.

With a smile of his own, he bent to talk to Eddie. “Whaddya think, Ed? A top-notch operation if I never saw one.”

Eddie barked once and let loose with a jubilant beagle howl. Zach resisted the urge to bust out with one of his own.

Violet was kneading the pie crust dough when Zach came into the diner Tuesday morning. She watched surreptitiously from the kitchen as he greeted his friends in the dining room. Bruises darkened his cheekbones and there was a bandage taped up high on his left temple. What could have happened, what almost happened, made her breath catch and she looked down quickly at the floury mass in her fingers. *Keep your mouth in check, Violet.*

This would be the challenge, she thought. Now that Beck was in jail along with Jones, her world would be her work, her old airport job, the diner…and Zach, but not in the way she yearned for.

I'll never find anyone like you.

Her admission had changed the tenor of their relationship, inserted an awkwardness between them that she'd have to live with. They'd go on joking, laughing, chatting, but behind the facade, he would know that she was in love with him, and she would always be reminded that he did not feel the same.

Get used to it. Zach was beginning to heal from the grief of his brother's murder, incrementally. She would continue to pray for

Jordy's killer to be caught, that Zach would open his heart to the Lord and inch by inch, he would take up the threads of his interrupted life…without her.

I hope you have peace, Zach, and rest and safety, just like the Psalm says. And that was the definition of love, she thought, wanting the best for Zach even if it couldn't be with her. Someday he would find that woman who would be a proper match for him, and Violet's heart would disintegrate, but she would never let on; she would always be the smiling, joking, tough-as-nails friend he wanted her to be.

Straightening her shoulders, she kneaded with more vigor.

"So that's how you stay in shape," Zach said as he tied an apron around his narrow waist. "Maybe I should try baking instead of lifting weights. I'm here to be your sous-chef like I promised."

"Oh, I forgot about our deal."

"Well, I didn't. Reporting for duty, Miss

Violet. Ready to slam-dunk this pie-making thing."

"You don't have to help. I can manage on my own."

"I am a man of my word when it comes to pastry. Quit stalling and show me the ropes."

Seeing that he was not about to be diverted, she retrieved a chilled disk of dough that she'd made earlier from the fridge, removed the plastic and put it on the floured stainless-steel counter in front of him. "We'll just take it one step at a time, Incinerator. Can you roll this out?"

"Of course I can. This is gonna be the best pie crust you ever tasted. People are going to line up around the block for a slice of this thing."

She sprinkled some flour on his rolling pin before she reached for the sugar and cornstarch and a saucepan to make the filling. She wished she had never made such a deal with Zach. It was too exquisitely painful to have him there, elbow to elbow with her, all jokes and banter and teasing as if they hadn't almost died together. He applied the rolling pin with enthusiasm.

"And anytime you're ready, you can show me how to do the scrambled egg thing. I am going to master that if it kills me."

"Right, as soon as there's free time," she said, intending never to initiate such a lesson unless he gave her no choice. She figured given his regular duties, his search to find Snapper and unearth Jordy's killer, combined with his natural restlessness, he would probably forget all about the egg-cooking lesson in time.

"You know, Vi," he said, working the rolling pin. "I've been thinking a lot about you."

She flipped her ponytail over her shoulder and forced a sassy reply. "Don't even start. I'm safe now. I'm going back to my job at LaGuardia on Monday, so there's no reason to bicker about that anymore."

He laughed as he continued his efforts with the pie dough. “But we’re so good at bickering, you and me. We’ve got it down pat. Everybody thinks so…you know, old married couple, like Jordy said.”

She looked up from her saucepan and eyed his progress. “Stop immediately,” she blurted.

“What?” he demanded. “This rolling is perfect.”

He had rolled the circle of dough into a colossal sheet of paper-thin pastry.

She could not hold back a giggle. “It’s gigantic. It’s supposed to fit a nine-inch pie.”

He surveyed his work. “Well, you didn’t tell me that.”

“Do I have to tell you everything?” When she reached for the rolling pin, he surprised her by circling her waist, pulling her close and turning her away from the pastry-covered counter.

“Yes, you do. You have to tell me everything, every little thing that’s on your mind, not just the stuff that you think it's okay to say."

She stared. "I don't understand. What are you talking about?"

"You're my best friend, Vi. There is no better qualification than that."

She wriggled in his arms. "Qualification for what?"

He turned her around then so she could see the engagement ring he'd placed in the middle of the dough. A white gold band set with a sparkling oval-cut diamond winked at her from its pastry background. It made not the slightest bit of sense no matter how long she ogled it. "Zach..."

He rocked her gently around so she would look at him again and away from the enigma. "I know, you think I'm stubborn and I break stuff and I don't admit when I'm wrong."

"Well, yes."

He laughed. "That's why I need a tough woman, a best friend who's not afraid to stand up to me." His smile trailed away and the expression left in its wake was tender and tremulous. "That's why I need you."

Need was the last word she'd expected from Zach Jameson. "You need me?"

He nodded. "In ways I never realized before."

"But you… I…we're friends. Aren't we?"

"Absolutely, best friends and we'll stay that way, but I finally figured out that it's not enough. I'm a really slow learner, but I get there eventually." He blew out a breath. "I love you, Vi. I want to marry you."

Something was taking place, something as monumental as an avalanche, as wide as a windswept sea, but she could not let her brain believe it. She felt desperate to back away from the dream unfolding before her. He spoke of love, for her, for them both, but she'd always loved him and he hadn't felt the same and it had been soul-crushing. She could not, must not, allow this fantasy to ruin either of them. "I… If this is about what I said, Zach…"

He grinned. "That you'd never find someone like me? Well you won't, and I'll never find anyone else like you, either."

"This is silly." She tried to push him away but he held her fast.

"You're gonna listen, Vi, so stop wiggling," he said again, a glint flashing through the sapphire of his eyes. "I'm the guy who's known you since you skinned your knees falling off your bike. I've raced you around the block, and trounced you, I might add. I helped you bandage your dolls and walked you home from school when you got sick in the lunchroom and I took care of the guy who teased you about it. And I let you bandage and splint me until I was mummified when you were working on your scout badge."

She opened her mouth to answer but he put a finger to her lips.

"And I'm the guy who knows that deep

down you are a world-class lady who is beautiful, loyal and faithful and who's gonna pray for me and our future kids even when we're too stubborn or broken to do it ourselves."

"Our future kids?"

He pressed his nose to her cheek and whispered. "Yeah. I'm thinking five, but I could round up if you want."

She could only gape at him as a tingling started up in her chest and spread throughout her limbs, lovely and light, like joy itself.

When he picked up the ring and slid it onto her flour-streaked finger, she had to blink against a wash of tears. Then he kissed her pinkie. "I'm that guy who will love you." He kissed the tip of her ring finger. "And take care of you." He kissed the next fingertip, and the next. "And drive you crazy and break your dishes." And then he kissed the top of her thumb. "And try my hardest every single day of my life to make you happy."

Dream or reality? How could it be the truth? Her pulse was thrumming so fast it radiated a frenetic pounding through her entire body, shaking her to the core, weakening the walls she'd built around her heart.

And then he sank to his knee on the floor, stirring up a cloud of flour that he'd spilled there.

"You'll ruin your clothes," she whispered.

"Oh yes, and break your crockery as we've discussed, but Vi, I will promise you right now that I will never break your heart. Will you marry me, Vi? Will you?" His expression clouded for a moment. "It won't be easy for a while, a long while, not until we catch Jordy's killer and find Snapper and even then..." He cleared his throat. "I have a lot of healing to do."

She touched a hand to his cheek, stroked a finger over the strong line of his jaw, soaked in the mingled joy and pain in his eyes. Joy and pain; there would be plenty of both ahead. This gorgeous, precious, darling man, the one whom she'd loved since she was a girl, her best friend, her defender, her love, had laid his soul bare and vulnerable at her feet. He looked at her with a love so true and pure that she knew it would last a lifetime. Finally, she allowed herself to believe, and bliss settled down on her with gossamer wings. She dropped to her knees next to him, there on the floor, and wrapped him in an embrace. "I love you, Zach. You were always the right one for me. Let's get married."

He shouted and squeezed her tight, his knees skidding on the floured floor.

"Just like Jordy always thought we would," he said, voice cracking only once as he found her mouth for the kiss she'd been waiting on her whole life long.

* * * * *

If you enjoyed Act of Valor,
look for Finn's story, Blind Trust,
coming up next, and the rest of the
True Blue K-9 Unit series
from Love Inspired Suspense.

TRUE BLUE K-9 UNIT:
These police officers fight for justice with
the help of their brave canine partners

Justice Mission *by Lynette Eason,*
April 2019
Act of Valor *by Dana Mentink, May 2019*
Blind Trust *by Laura Scott, June 2019*
Deep Undercover *by Lenora Worth,*
July 2019
Seeking the Truth *by Terri Reed,*
August 2019
Trail of Danger *by Valerie Hansen,*
September 2019

Courage Under Fire *by Sharon Dunn,*
October 2019
Sworn to Protect *by Shirlee McCoy,*
November 2019
True Blue K-9 Unit Christmas
by Laura Scott and Maggie K. Black,
December 2019

Dear Reader,

I hope you enjoyed meeting Zach, Violet and Eddie, the beagle. It was great fun to write about their adventures in the big city. Beagles are pretty fascinating animals. Their name comes from the French and means "wide throat" or "loudmouth," which is fitting due to their irrepressible baying. Originally, beagles were bred to be very small dogs, small enough to fit in a pocket, but now they range in size from fourteen to sixteen inches tall. President Lyndon Johnson owned two beagles named Him and Her. The Department of Homeland Security employs a "Beagle Brigade" to sniff out contraband in agricultural products.

While Eddie is the canine star, his handler, Zach, and Violet risk their lives to take some drug dealers off the streets. They have to come to terms with their own weaknesses and erroneous perceptions of each other to realize that they were meant to be together. Their future is bright because God has helped them to be best friends before they will become husband and wife. What a perfect recipe for a relationship!

I hope you have enjoyed this next installment in the True Blue K-9 series. The saga unfolds in the next book as the hunt for Jordan Jameson's killer continues. You can be sure that there will be thrilling twists and turns ahead for the K-9 officers and their incredible dog partners! As always, I love to hear from my readers. If you'd like to contact me, you can find me on the usual cyber stops (Facebook, Twitter, Instagram) and via my website at www.danamentink.com. There is a physical address listed on my website for those who prefer to correspond by mail. Thank you again for coming along on this journey. God bless you, friends!

Sincerely,

Dana Mentink